HIDING PLACE
AT
BARRINGTON HALL

A NOVEL
BY
MARY ELLEN GAVIN

DEDICATION

This work of fiction is dedicated to the men and women who labor in the medical profession: doctors, nurses, CNAs and all the other medical specialists who guide and repair us during birth, illness, disease and death.

Acknowledgements

My love-of-story developed in our kitchen where I was able to listen to a variety of people recounting their lives, their loves, their losses. Quiet talks, especially with our nonjudgmental mother, were as safe there as in any confessional.

My older sisters were film buffs, long before the term was coined, and often took me to the movies. The stories, playing out on the big screen, filled me with wonder and still do to this day. I am grateful to my sisters for sharing this gift and I am in awe of filmmakers.

I was blessed with fine teachers who utilized the art of storytelling to enrich our school subjects from arithmetic to spelling. They dusted off historical figures to bring them back to life so we could envision each one as being human again. Our learned educators accomplished this through their research of back story.

Most of all, I must acknowledge the authors who toiled before me. Their works opened my mind. Brave writers spent countless hours to describe characters and arch types and situations that might never have been told without their brilliance and without their taking pen to paper.

I personally thank anyone who ever trusted me with their whispered or written tales of good, bad or indifference. And, of course, I love all those who have ever read, listened, reviewed, or edited my words and they will go straight to heaven.

Thank you, one and all!

HIDING PLACES AT BARRINGTON HALL

Chapter One

The day Pat Hannelly and I formed Hannelly & Hennessey Investigations was bittersweet. Being widows whose husbands had succumbed to illness and died young, we were left with sons in college and mortgages. After the fog of mourning lifted, we conspired over a bottle of wine and drew up a plan to be private detectives even though the idea scared the hell out of me.

We took the classes, got through the background investigations and we were licensed by the Commonwealth of Virginia. The next step: promote the new enterprise. Our first marketing campaign was modeled for the federal government where our husbands had been employed. Finding contract work naturally fell to Pat as she was the epitome of a social butterfly and the perfect Marketing Manager. Her quick smile and easy manner inspired trust. And we agreed that trust was our selling point and the foundation of how we would do business.

I took on the position of Operations Manager. It would be my duty to secure clean paperwork for the contract and get a clear understanding of the customer requirements. On-time deliverables were mandatory when working for any government agency as they were on the clock to report cost and progress internally.

Not long after starting our business venture, Pat and I were cruising the rainy streets of Georgetown at three in the morning. It was garbage night. The high class residents, politicos and university types, had set out their cans filled with tidy plastic bags.

Pat's sleek truck rolled past the fancy addresses while I scanned our list of pick-up orders and she searched street signs and townhouse numbers. Garbage Runs, as they were lovingly called, were our most requested jobs. Contracts arrived from a *variety* of clients, who wanted to see a *variety* of trash, for a *variety* of reasons which were never explained.

As Pat maneuvered along Wisconsin Avenue, I pulled on my black latex gloves and wondered aloud, "Are we the only fools who'll do these scavenger jobs?"

When Pat turned her head to smile at me, her trademark ponytail full of shiny brown hair swayed across her shoulders. "Don't knock it, Meg. This grunt work brings in cash and bumps up our reputation. Competition for investigative work is stiff. I don't need to tell you that every government worker dreams of starting a contractor business." She gave me another bright smile and threw a soft punch into my shoulder. "And, here we are living the dream!"

We chuckled until I questioned why we were pulling so much trash out of Georgetown. "Do I smell a political scandal?" It was a rhetorical question that she never answered because there was always a political scandal brewing in the Capitol.

Laughing with Pat, I was reminded of the first day we met. We stepped into the dark classroom for first grade at St. Thomas School in Fairfax County. Checking the wall clock, we laughed, realizing we had arrived too early on our first day as teacher aides. And while we sat in the tiny chairs, we revealed why we were volunteering. I pointed to the school being overcrowded and the teachers being overworked. She added, "And don't forget, they toil under the iron rule of our strict Gaelic pastor."

Joking together and staying close over the years, Pat and I prevailed while other school volunteers ran screaming out the door. We supported each other at school and it helped that our husbands worked for the same federal agency. As our sons rose through their eight years to graduation, sitting close in alpha order, our two families gained a lasting friendship.

Pat Hannelly was tough in a funny sort of way. She had early on found her inner strength as an Army brat and loved to use her drill-sergeant voice. The children enjoyed her playfulness, but respected her command. Pat became a warrior when a person of authority took advantage of their positions. Her favorite side remark to me was, "Screw with one of us? They screw with both of us!"

Pat Hannelly was resilient and stood up for what was just, especially if she felt something was not fair for a student or a teacher. She picked up her sword and took up their battles rarely losing even against our self-righteous pastor. Those conflicts did not go unnoticed, especially by some of the office clerical and church women who delighted in gossip. At the graduation dinner, we toasted our years of service. Privately, we acknowledged in whispers that we were probably *persona non gratis* in the parish and might have set a bad example for future teacher aides.

Holding up her glass, she twisted her ever-present smile into a frown and impersonated the pompous pastor. Stomping her foot, she pretended to spit on the floor. "That's what I think of those Two "H" Women!" After our laughter she looked sad. "Hey Meg, didn't you hate that the holier-than-thou jackass who preached charity never tried to remember our names?"

"Don't let it bother you." I saw her hurt and fibbed. "He's only covering for his dementia."

Hearing our husbands praising the old pastor, I walked over with Pat on my heels and interrupted. "Don't you fellas admire that man because he hails from the Old Sod. We may not have complained to you, but our lives were made miserable over the years by that man."

Pat took over. "He was the crazy person who started that awful innuendo about young Father Paul." She had their attention now. "That young man came here after years of prison duty. He was so happy to be in a family parish and didn't that Irish bastard start rumors. Yeah, rumors that Father Paul was too friendly with the females. How sad was that day when our young priest got booted out on his behind to go find another parish!" The men never flattered the pastor again.

Over the years, Pat and I had stood up to the tensions at school and being married to high-energy husbands who worked in the intelligence arena. Still, we hardly made it through the onset of their sudden illnesses that only led to death. Pat consoled me over the loss of Bill and not long after her husband, Neil, succumbed to the ravages of another killer disease.

The two "H" women lost social standings and privileges upon entering widowhood. Invitations to fancy dinners and stylish lunches organized by the power people stopped coming. Those who pledged never to forget us stopped calling. Our presence was no longer required at the Washington Galas or Kennedy Center Celebrations.

One morning while I was rocking in my new favorite chair, I spotted Pat running up to the door. Glad to see her, I let her in and saw that she was in a classy blue exercise outfit.

"C'mon in, Pat. You look great! Are those new shoes?"

"Yep. And this is for you." She handed me a large bag. "We're going to the gym."

I tried to back away from the idea, but there was no saying NO to Patricia Hannelly when she had her mind made up. Plus, I caught a sparkle in her brown eyes: her wicked tell.

Eager for her company, I agreed to change into the new clothes. We went up to my bedroom and she sounded excited that we would take up exercise again. I agreed, but worried that going back to our old club might include some form of *retaliation*.

When we arrived, I hesitated at the door. "I don't know if I want to see all those gawking women who dumped us as soon as we were no longer a couple."

"Screw them! We're not the same crying widows they saw at the funeral parlor."

Her conviction made me blink away my tears. "Are you sure?"

"Listen, I've got a plan to get us up and going." She smiled. "For now, throw your head back and act as if you've got it all together. Pretend we have secret lovers."

"How the hell do I do that?"

She stood straight and bounced forward on her new gyms. I watched her pony tail shake as she led the way. Strutting in the door, we pretended to giggle over nothing. Heads turned to stare. Embarrassed faces showed recognition and turned away to wag their tongues. Signing in at the desk, we got a locker key and dumped our purses in the little steel cubbies.

Following Pat's lead, I stretched muscles that had been frozen after so many months of inertia. Fake smiles covered our small outbursts of pain until we could finally endure the exercise. While bending down, bouncing on our feet, Pat laid out her plan. "I was at my wit's end, trying to come up with a moneymaker where you and I could keep our independence."

"I thought about asking the agency to hire me. They provide hardship jobs for widows, but the thought of begging for work made me feel sad."

Pat gave me her look of disgusted. "Get that bee out of your bonnet."

"Love when you use old expressions." I tried to appease her, "but put that idea on your job opportunity list just in case."

"Yeah, on the bottom after bank robbery and suicide." She broke out in a smile. "I'm thinking we can open a private investigator operation. There's lots of low-level work we could scrounge from the agencies. They already have files worked up on us and know we're trustworthy. Besides, they love handing out contracts to women-owned businesses."

I stopped stretching to ask, "How the hell do we become investigators?"

"I found a school run by a top guy in the field who's ex-agency. He'll provide the training and the exam in his office right here in Northern Virginia. And he doesn't want a lot of money. What do you think, partner?"

The idea of being detectives ran through my head and to my surprise, I liked it. But there were drawbacks. "Does this entail karate kicks, hidden daggers and gun fights?

"Could be?" Pat flashed her brown eyes. "Which is why we forty-somethings need to get into shape. And today's the first step." She heard my groan and put her arm around me. "Give us a few months. We'll stick to a regime and feel like thirty-somethings soon. I guarantee it!"

True to her word, five months later we presented ourselves as years younger, energetic and in shape. During those months, we went to investigator school and learned the lessons. We listened to the stories from other P.I.s and passed the licensing exam. There was not one physical course that we backed away from and did fairly well ... for girls, or so said our male instructors.

Shooting handguns? That was another story. Pat and I quickly realized that we had eye defects which sent us to the ophthalmologist. She opted for laser surgery while I consented to contact lenses. We were still way off target at the gun range. The other shooters who were mostly male ... mostly agency, military and police chided us. Still, we stood toe-to-toe with them. Guns drawn, firing away, we did not back off until we put a hole somewhere inside that circle to their chagrin and applause.

We were even allowed to run the pop-up course with live ammo. One at a time, each runner made his or her way through the maze of mechanical cardboard figures that could come from nowhere. Some were innocent, some were would-be-killers. Being timed for the course, forced the competitor to go for speed and accuracy. All the while those waiting, before or after their turn, got to watch the competitors on closed circuit monitors.

I was cautious on my run, being very sure before I took aim and fired. My hesitance did not serve me well. Long before I made it to the end, a pop-up of a blind man in cool sunglasses walking his seeing-eye bulldog stopped me in my tracks. I froze, not knowing what to do. In that instant, white flour shot out at me from the life-size figure before I could get a shot off. The roar of laughter reached out to me before I opened the door to the waiting room. Pat ran up, laughing as the gun shop owner hollered, "A seeing-eye BULLDOG walking without a leash didn't give it away?" The crowd roared and I raised my hands in defeat.

Pat choked on her laughter and when she regained control I said, "Go make us proud!"

I stood with the group and watched the screen. Pat entered the reformed course and showed her innate sense of stealth by slowing down as she neared the hidden bad guys. Keeping control over her trigger finger, she kept going when the innocent appeared and made kill shots when her life was in danger. Pat was the only one to fire upon the ugly nun clutching the swaddled newborn that turned out to be a man in drag, holding a cocked gun under a doll. She earned the biggest applause and pats on the back for the day.

Needing to speed up my own progress, I ran that course several times over the next few weeks with different characters set up to bounce out at me until I finally caught up to her accuracy and time. These were memories that I would never forget.

As we slid along the wet streets I asked Pat, "So, what brings us to Georgetown?"

"It's a mystery." Hitting the brake for a red light, she reached for her purse and handed over a piece of paper tucked inside a plastic bag. "This was waiting at our mail box with a thousand bucks in Benjamins. What do you think?"

Turning the evidence bag in my hands, I was able to read the printed note asking us to pick up and sift the garbage at a Georgetown address for the next week. "It's not signed, only a phone number if we find something unusual." Still wiping raindrops off my face from our last stop, I asked if she had run the phone number?

"It's off the grid. I couldn't locate it even with our expensive software. I didn't bother calling it as we may not have anything to report. Then, we'll just keep the money."

"I wonder what their definition of unusual might be?" Looking up, I Spotted the side street listed on the note and pointed it out to Pat.

She made a quick left and slowed down. The sleepy street lined with million dollar townhouses was empty of moving traffic. Pat stopped the truck and turned off her headlights.

Since reconnaissance and retrieval were my jobs to be done on foot, I jumped out. When my black canvas shoes hit the slimy pavement, the slippery blacktop sent me sliding into the tail end of a parked Jaguar. Stepping across the grass, I moved up the sidewalk until my tired eyes spotted a set of door numbers that I could barely see in the dark. Figuring that our mark's address had to be a block down, I signaled to Pat to slow roll alongside me. I jogged the block in my black suit with the hood up to cover my hair and face.

Sliding to a stop at the precise address, I saw that the coveted garbage was already waiting at the curb. Creeping up to the can, I lifted the bags, but they were heavy. When I had all three in my grip, I heard the squeak of the truck's passenger door being pushed open. Pat was readying for my reentry.

At the same time, I felt a wet nose sniffing around my ankles. Looking down, I saw a strange little dog with what looked like a Pit Bull head with pointy ears attached to a small Terrier body. To add to this mutt's oddity, his silver coat was a grey and white mix.

"Hurry, someone's coming!" Pat whispered in her low, excited, voice.

Before I could respond, a strong male voice hollered out from the back of the building. "Silver! Where the hell are you? You better not be in the alley, chasing those damn cats again?"

When the front porch lit up, I knew Pat would accelerate up the street according to our prearranged protocol. I watched as she moved away so as not to bring attention to her idling truck. At the cross street she would turn and wait, while I ran my ass off to catch up with her.

I began to jog, but my shoes kept sliding. Still holding the trash bags in front of me, I caught my stride. My feet kept running until I realized that my new friend was right beside me. "Daddy's calling. Go home, Silver!"

Now, I could hear his master's voice calling out from the front of the house. When I turned to sneak a look at the shadow of a broad shouldered man standing several houses behind me, I lost sight of Pat's truck. There was no sign of her and I faced a long run to the cross street. Passing under a street light, I looked down for the dog. Silver was still with me. While I wondered if I could outrun him, his master called out again.

This time, Silver obeyed. He stopped and watched as I ran forward. Breathing easier, I did not miss the sound of Silver's little paws running beside me. Ready to get off this street, I lengthened my stride not knowing whether Silver's master was chasing me or not. After all, I had taken his trash bags. My heart kept racing and I could no longer hear because my ears were buzzing. As my feet hit the curb, I spotted the waiting truck to my right.

Skidding along the blacktop, I threw the bags into the open backend and tried to slide around the rear of the truck to the passenger side. Pat was leaning over, opening the door for me. Before I could reach it, my feet slipped out from under me. At first, my body flew backwards. Trying to right myself midair, I leaned forward. Completely off balance, my full weight went down on my right knee and I slid into the open door. All the stars in the universe shined for me..

Pat looked down at me squatting on the pavement. While my mind traveled outer space, my partner gathered me up and pushed my dead weight into the passenger seat. The last I heard were her dual mufflers blowing exhaust.

Waking up in D.C. Community's ER, I looked up at a nurse cutting off my pants with the precision of a Sushi chef. She gave both of us the once over and turned up her nose. "Whew, you ladies stink like garbage. What alleys have you been working in tonight?"

Pat laughed, "My friend slipped in the rain and fell into a garbage can."

I slowly formed the words necessary to ask, "What's wrong with my knee?"

The nurse bent her head close to my face and I watched her ruby red lips. "Looks like you ripped your Patella to shreds."

Chapter Two

Waking up in a dark hospital room, I looked out the window. I must have been on a high floor as I could see the Capitol's cityscape. Rooftop images showed the sun setting behind the old buildings so rich in history. Watching the last of daylight disappear, a wave of agony washed over me. My injured leg felt numb and would not move, but I felt the worst was over.

A soft pinging sound caught my attention and I searched for its source as it continued to get louder. Without contacts, it was difficult to follow the tiny alarm to the mechanical drip. Sitting up on my elbow, I saw a male nurse walk in followed by Pat. She carried a steaming cup of her favorite drive-thru coffee and looked tired. She gave me a big smile. "Hey, you're awake?"

My mouth was dry. I pulled away the plastic oxygen tubes winding around my face to ask, "How long have I been here?" The syllables crackled from my sore throat.

Pat bent over to look into my eyes. "Two days." She winced. "How do you feel?"

"Like cat crap. How do I look?"

"Like run-over cat crap."

"Tell me the fall was worth it. Did you sift through those three garbage bags?"

"Yep! The cleanest trash I've ever seen. A male living with his dog, nothing more."

"The *dog* would be my new friend, Silver?"

"The one and only!"

 "That little canine is a fast runner."

"You are lucky. Silver is a Pit Bull mix and could have taken a bite out of you."

Looking down at the blue brace strapped to the length of my leg, I sighed. "Yeah, good thing the dog left me alone so I could keep running, fall and break my knee."

"I'm sorry you went down." Pat made her sad face.

I waved off her pity. "Back to the trash, was there anything?"

"No signs of a female, or a smoker, or a drinker. Silver and his master lead a clean life, eat the finest food out of cartons from the best restaurants around town."

"Any more envelopes with money show up at our P.O. box?"

"No, but I'm still curious about that phone number."

"Sorry I can't help you for awhile. You know I'd rather be working than in here."

"Bone Doc said your surgery was successful. He wired your knee." Pat looked worried.

"Tell me the truth. What's the bad news?"

"Listen Meg, your knee is going to take a long time to heal." She pointed to my brace. "They have you in an Immobilizer from your hip to your ankle so you can't move it."

"Okay. What's so awful about that?"

"You're gonna be in it for at least eight weeks."

I felt a wave of nausea. "I have to be in bed all that time?"

"Worse, you're going to be in rehab for all that time."

My brain could not wrap around her concern. "Why can't I just go home?"

"To an empty house?" She frowned, "Or, should your son ditch college to care for you?"

I shook my head. "No, of course not. I don't want that, but...."

"I talked to him. He's willing to come home. Almost too willing?"

We both laughed, but I still wondered, "Couldn't I take care of myself?"

"No! You can't put weight on your leg or it's back to surgery."

I could feel my body slump in resignation. "Tell me about rehab. How hard could it be?"

Pat waited for the nurse changing the I.V. bags to leave before giving me one of her wicked smiles. "Rainey says this is a golden opportunity ... you needing to go to a facility."

I took a breath. Pat Hannelly was our marketing guru, always looking to sell our services. She had recently mentioned making contact with Luc Raines, a man we only knew by reputation as a high-ranking spook from one of the darker agencies. Hearing his name made my stomach quiver. "Pat, what've you gotten us into?"

"Don't worry!" She whispered. "I know what I'm doing. Luc's a nice guy. He admits that we can't get on board for most of his operations cause they're stealth or overseas or both. But, he says if we take on this job, he'll pay us handsomely and give us more work than we can handle. Just think." She let a sly smile cross her lips. "We could get an office and hire investigators!"

The sparks of enthusiasm shooting out of her eyes frightened me. I got up on both elbows to convey my reluctance. "Please don't get us into any of that man's monkey business."

"What have you heard?"

"Luc Raines is a Heavy Breather answering to no one. He's a Dirty Tricks Guy; not to be trusted. I hope you are not being too sweet with him?"

Pat bit her lip, always a sign that she had alternate views that she was keeping to herself. "So far, it's all business. Luc says he knew Neal and ... I'm playing the poor-widow card."

"And, what do *we* have to do for this contract he's offering us?"

She shook her head. "He can't give us paper on this one, but I trust that he'll pay us."

"Okay, what do we have to do for *his promise* to pay us?"

"You're going to be transported to Barrington Hall in Virginia. I scouted it out while you were in surgery. It's a beautiful place high up on the cliffs overlooking the Potomac River. Luc'll give us our assignment once you get there."

Exhaustion forced me to fall back on my pillow and close my eyes.

She patted my shoulder. "Don't worry, it's only an eyes-and-ears job. See ya tomorrow."

The next time I opened my eyes, Pat was gone and my knee was on fire. I clicked the morphine drip and waited for relief. As the narcotic swam into my bloodstream, I worried about performing any kind of work for Luc Raines. Since Langley was only commissioned to work covertly outside our country, I reconciled that this request should not be dangerous. Still, I doubted whether Pat was thinking past the man's handsome features that I had only heard about.

Falling into a dark abyss, I saw the face of my dead husband. He looked worried, as if he was trying to tell me something, but his lips never moved. As his image faded, I remembered a curious thing. Bill had often mentioned how leery he was of status-seeking government types who were often appointees. He was especially wary of the Princeton and Yale boys and I wondered which Ivy League school heralded Raines as one of their graduates.

HIDING PLACES AT BARRINGTON HALL

Chapter Three

If I had not been strapped down to the gurney, I would have sat up in the ambulance to survey the rehabilitation complex known as Barrington Hall. As we turned off Georgetown Pike and headed up the private road to it, I felt a sense of dread. Speeding past the open gate, my stomach did flip-flops. I had often wondered what was behind this tall iron fence passing it so many times on my way to Great Falls. Little did I ever expect to be delivered here for a long stay.

When we stopped under the big overhang, medical personnel greeted the driver and assistant. I heard my name being introduced and permission was given to enter the building. The two young men wheeled me out of the ambulance and elevated the stretcher so I could be easily pushed through the entranceway. My sense of the place was more like a palatial mansion than a medical center. The windows were large allowing lots of sunlight to shine on the pastel walls. Soft versions of current music played from ceiling speakers.

Stopping at the Nurse's Station that looked as if it was built three steps above the floor, two nurses in white stood smiling. The blonde grabbed my hand. "Welcome Meg, we've been waiting for you. You're in room 112. Your partner's Margaret Sanderson." The other nurse handed a clipboard to the ambulance attendant and he signed it before pushing me forward.

From what I could tell the corridors were laid out in a letter H configuration. The Nurse's Station and elevators were in the center hall connecting the two long ones. Room 112 was bright blue with flowered wallpaper. An empty bed wearing crisp blue linen awaited me. My eyes lit up to see that it was next to a window. I laughed, thinking how I could use the fairly large portal to escape ... but only if I could walk. After the attendants got me settled, they bid me farewell.

I craned my neck to peek around the dividing curtain that separated the two spaces and saw dozens of photos and cards hanging on Margaret Sanderson's side of the room. Seeing her family's pictures and cards of love, I realized that she had been here for a long while.

While I labored over learning how to use the controller to operate the bed positions and call button, Mr. Sanderson wheeled Margaret into the room. They were a sweet looking couple in their eighties, both with full heads of silvery white hair. They greeted me warmly and I liked them immediately. Laying back, I relaxed as Mr. Sanderson explained how Margaret had fallen and injured her neck. She let him do the talking and I loved the smooth sound of his voice.

I listened as he recounted their life together until two young ladies dressed in blue scrubs came in to see me. With wide smiles they presented themselves as my Certified Nursing Assistants. The black beauty made the introductions. "I'm Mary and this is Lyrie," she pointed to the petite gal who looked like a teenager even though she was showing.

Lyrie spelled out her first name, "L Y R I C A L!" She went on to explain, "My mother said the sound of my newborn cry was lyrical. "Everyone calls me, Lyrie." She patted my hand, "What do you want us to call you?"

"You can call me, Meg."

Mary added, "We'll make you comfortable while you get used to the routine." She looked down at my leg still wrapped tight in the Immobilizer. "Oh, oh! You're going to need a commode, or would you prefer a bed pan?"

"What's a commode?"

Lyrie winked, "A chair with a pot under the lid. Say yes, it's much better than bedpans."

"Anything's better than bedpans." We all laughed and I took them to be friends.

The rest of the afternoon was taken up with filling out a menu for my dinner tray that would be served to my rolling bed table. The typed piece of paper listed a variety of dishes and when the dinner tray arrived, it was presented in an appetizing manner. The small portions were tasty and filling. Since this was the first time that my food had not been delivered through a plastic tube, it was a good beginning.

Later in the evening, personnel in civilian clothes came to the end of my bed and talked about what the facility had to offer. Most of what they mentioned went over my groggy head and they knew it. All I could do was ask about pain meds as my knee felt as if it was going to explode. One of the ladies tried to explain how there was a beauty shop downstairs, but finally gave up and promised to send in the nurse.

My angel of mercy wearing the name tag, Angela, ran in with a tiny plastic cup full of pills. "Since you received so many heavy drugs at the hospital, my instructions were to wait until you asked. We'll establish a schedule so you don't have extreme pain. When you're ready, we'll back away until we get to where you'll have to request pain relief. Sound good?"

I warmed to her plan and I liked her dimpled smile. "Sounds wonderful, Angela!"

It was not long before my eyelids fluttered. Mr. Sanderson was narrating the opening to a TALE OF TWO CITIES on the other side of the center curtain, His smooth oratory, meant only for wife, swept me away to the Paris that Charles Dickens described before the peasant storm of rebellion. My drugged mind could visualize the characters as if they were from my own lifetime.

After several hours of dreamless sleep, I awoke startled. Someone was moving toward my bed. As the shadow settled atop the closed commode next to the window, I heard a soft voice whisper. "It's me. Stay quiet. It's after visiting hours."

I sat up. Seeing Pat's sweet features bathed in moonlight calmed my heartbeat. She was dressed in blue scrubs and before I could question them, her palm pushed against my lips

"I sneaked in with the arriving CNAs during the late shift change."

She removed her hand so I was able to whisper back, "Why the cloak and dagger?"

"This case has become *more* complicated."

"Don't even try to explain. I won't get it. I'm still not thinking straight."

"We'll talk tomorrow. I've brought a small traveling case. It's special." She raised a black canvas bag that looked ordinary. "The top has toiletries, but there's a false bottom." She stood and pushed it inside my oak wardrobe. Before she got it situated, the Call Light began flashing.

We both jumped and Pat turned to leave. "I gotta get out of here."

I spoke up, "Mrs. Sanderson, did you call for a nurse?"

"Yes dear, I have to go to the toilet," she answered sleepily.

Pat scooted into the darkened hallway only seconds before our attending CNA entered.

Chapter Four

My first morning at Barrington Hall began at daybreak with the facility's janitorial workers, dressed in maroon scrubs, mopping the floors under our beds. They hummed while dropping off clean linens and refreshing our carafes with water and ice. More of the maroons followed them in pushing wet mops. They were a happy group and I relaxed. Falling back asleep, it was not until a breakfast menu was waved in front of my face that I opened my eyes again.

Mary's warm smile stopped any complaint I might have wanted to make. "You're going to be fussed with today." Her eyes opened wide. "Better wake up, clean up and get dressed. Every person in this place is about to come here to talk with you."

"Put on my own clothes? You're kidding. How can I do that with this leg brace?"

I'll help you after you eat, but then you're on your own. This is not a spa." She laughed heartily, strutting her behind out the door and leaving me to scowl.

The scrambled eggs and bacon tasted wonderful. As soon as Mary took away my breakfast tray, she returned with a small tub of water. "I'll pull the curtain so the Sandersons don't have to come back from the cafeteria and see you all naked." Her uppity manner made me laugh, but I did everything that she told me to do. Mary was right. The warm moist cloth against my skin felt wonderful. And, dusting on my favorite perfumed powder almost made me feel human again. I felt so rejuvenated that I stretched my arm out and reached into my wardrobe. There was a pair of sweat pants with only one left leg. Pat must have taken the scissors to it.

After getting on all of my clothes, I heard my name being called from the hallway. A shadow of a short female loomed beyond the drawn curtain. At first, I did not answer.

"Meg Hennessey, I know you're in there. Knock! Knock! Can I open up?" Before I had a chance to answer, the sheer curtain drawn around my bed flew around the ceiling track. There stood a beautiful young woman with big brown eyes. She wore a tight black polo and beige khakis. Her hand gripped a wheel chair already setup with the right leg going straight out.

"I'm Cheryl, one of your physical therapists." She did not wait for my response. "We'll work together on your upper body to make sure you stay strong while you're here. Hop in the chair." Her sweet voice was turning sour. "C'mon, time's a wasting. Let's get going!"

My icy stare was meant to stop her cold. When it did not work, I shouted."I'm only here to let my leg heal."

She squinted and said, "Oh no, don't think you're going to lounge in that bed. Your insurance company insists that you get physical therapy five days a week, or guess what?" She did not wait for my response. Instead, she put her hands on her hips and smirked. "They won't honor your claim. You'll be paying the Hotel Barrington for your stay here. Let's go!"

"I can't. Get out of here and leave me alone."

She jammed the wheelchair up to my bed and looked mad. "Get in!"

Picturing the insurance company not picking up my hefty tab, I thought better of promoting my independence any further until I got this straightened out with the facility. I scooted my backside across the mattress as she lowered the bed until it was even with the chair. Moving my body into the chair was a struggle because I could not lift the dead weight in the brace. She finally held up my right leg until I flopped into the wheel chair.

"Now, wasn't that easy." Her features wrinkled up into a told-you-so face.

My blood boiled and angry thoughts began to swim in my head. "I feel dizzy."

"Try NOT to vomit. Now, let's GO!" She turned and started for the door.

"I'm still weak from surgery. Aren't you going to push me?" I was telling the truth.

Without stopping she hollered back, "No, you need all the exercise you can get."

I grasped the rubber wheels and began to push. Maneuvering around Margaret's bed was not easy, but I finally made it into the hallway. The bright ceiling lights hitting my eyes made me feel even sicker. I stopped pushing and called out. "I'm nauseous."

Cheryl turned around, but appeared more interested in checking out her fingernails than my sick stomach. "It'll pass." She stood and waited for me to pick up speed again.

"I want to go back to bed."

"Not an option. Let's GO."

I pushed a few feet further to the end of the corridor and stopped. She turned and disappeared while I was left trying to figure out how to make a turn in a wheelchair. With no help from Cheryl, it registered that I could only push one wheel to make the chair turn in the opposite direction. Catching up I yelled to her, "Thanks a lot, Nurse Ratchette!"

"That's not my name and you know it."

"It is as far as I'm concerned. By the way, where is this gym?"

"Keep going to the end of this hall and make another left."

"We're going in circles. I'll puke for sure!"

"You're doing fine. Stop complaining!"

"My knee hurts like hell. You're aggravating it!"

"See all the wheelchairs lined up by the big door on the right. That's the gym."

All I saw were poor slobs like me groaning and moaning to other staff members also dressed in black polos and beige slacks. We were all being herded inside and it made me angry. Not just for myself but for all of us. I cried out, "How can we exercise when we're all broken?"

"I'm not going to listen to your whining, Meg." Cheryl called back.

"Ms. Hennessey to you." I hated that I was no longer a Mrs. and I hated that woman.

Impatient with my slow pace, Cheryl stepped back and pushed me into line with the others. We were a pitiful lot dressed in large bandages or braces. A few were missing limbs.   Getting me inside, Cheryl parked my chair between the parallel bars and the wooden staircase before disappearing. I did not care where she went and hoped Cheryl would never return. Still upset, my belly juices began to boil and make threatening noises.

Looking around at the other infirmed still lining up, I realized how bad off we all were without the use of one or more of our appendages. And yet, my wounds would mend and I would recover. Most sitting around me were elderly and obese. We began to talk freely about our ailments. Diabetes was the culprit so often blamed for their weight gain, poor eyesight and falls. It was also the number one reason why their limbs had been surgically removed.

The woman sitting next to me with bright eyes and beautiful features did a change-up on our stories of how we got there. She began telling us her funny stories about her life. When she talked, I could see that her bottom front teeth were missing. I tried to look away, but my eyes would not stop watching the tip of her tongue slip in and out of her dental gap.

As the others were moved to their workout stations, she started up a conversation with me. "My name's Darlene. Looks like you and I are the youngest here." Her head spun around the gym checking out the other patients in order to bona fide her statement. Confident, she turned to me and asked, "I see ya hurt your leg. Someone push ya down?"

I was taken back but said, "My knee cap gets mad all over again when I discuss it."

Darlene began to laugh, a deep smoker's laugh, and I knew that I liked her. She stopped laughing, but kept her smile when she told me about her accident. "I took a header out in the garage. Laid there with a broken tibia for four hours while my grown son watched the football game. Can ya believe that?"

"Sure I can. Must've been a good game. Who was playing?"

Darlene laughed again, "Hey, you're a pistol. What's your name?"

"Meg, nice to meet you." I reached out and shook her hand.

Darlene moved closer. "What do you think of the physical therapists here?"

"I've only met Cheryl and she stings like a nest of wasps.

"None of 'em have a heart. They like to deliver pain. I'm going to need a pain pill."

Her big eyes bugged out. "As soon as you get back to your room, beg the nurse for one. And never come here sober again. Meds before and after PT, or you'll go crazy."

Cheryl brought hand weights to both of us. Together, Darlene and I pushed them forward, upward and sideways. We puffed until our faces turned red. Cheryl would not let us stop until we finished every rep as counted out by her. When our Task Master got pulled away or chatted to the other therapists, Darlene pushed up our count and I giggled. Cheryl squinted at us in disbelief, but when she walked away again Darlene upped the count again, "Hell with her!"

And when Cheryl turned her skinny ass around and walked away to fetch more tools of her trade, I stuck out my tongue while Darlene flipped her the bird.

Chapter Five

I fell asleep the second night without my sedative. I planned to delay taking it as I wanted to be alert when Pat arrived. I used my tongue to tuck the tiny pill between my gums and cheek when it was presented and pretended to swallow it. When the nurse left, I hid it under my pillow.

Without the sedative, my mind kept reenacting the fall when I went to sleep. As if going over it again and again would reboot that part of my brain in control of balance. In a light trance, I felt my feet slip out from under me and I jumped off the pillow.

Looking around, I spotted Pat's shadow once again sitting on my commode. She turned from looking at the night's stars and whispered. "Bad dream?"

"I want to go home."

"That won't stop your mind from replaying that nasty fall."

Wiping the perspiration from my brow, I tried to explain. "It's this place. I hate it here."

"Tell me what you hate here and we'll make a formal complaint to fix it."

Silence waited for my answer and I said, "There's one bitch in therapy."

"Is she working with your top or bottom half?"

"Top half, but she made me wheel myself into the gym this morning."

"You have to work to keep your upper body strength?"

My voice squeaked as I feebly protested. "Are you on her side?"

The sound of another voice broke in and we stopped to listen. It was Mrs. Sanderson tossing in her bed and moaning. "Oh, Ernie! That feels so wonderful."

Pat and I giggled until she whispered, "Lucky lady's enjoying a sweet dream of her husband." Pat's smile faded and she turned back to gaze out the window. "I made a wish for us."

I sighed, knowing her wish for us could never come true.

We stared at the starry sky for a few moments before pat looked back at me. This time she looked serious. "Rainey explained the setup here."

I stopped her. "Pat, let's not take on this job. Honestly, I'm not up to it."

"Don't worry, it'll be easy."

"I always worry when someone tells me not to worry." We both laughed at my old cliché. "No really, I mean it. Let's leave this one alone. I've got a cold feeling about this place. All I want to do is let my leg heal and get the hell out of here."

"Okay, but will you hear me out?"

I waved my hand. "Shoot!"

Pat leaned close. "There's a physical therapist here who as a young man allied with the agency during the last year of the Cold War. Beck is his name and he won the agency's gratitude for passing information out of the Soviet Union. As a reward, he received a no-questions-asked approval for dual citizenship between Poland and the U.S."

"So what's our assignment here?"

"Rainey wants you to contact this Beck and he'll give you a heads-up."

"So much damn intrigue!" I sighed, "I suppose there's a code word I'm supposed to use?"

Pat smiled, "Nah, Beck's been briefed and knows you're here. Your first challenge will be to get him as your therapist. He's reputed to be maniacal and demanding with his patients, but a miracle worker for leg injuries. He's in demand so it won't be easy."

"It'll be tough. The gym's full of fall-victims wearing leg braces just like me."

"Have you spotted him yet?"

"Not that I recall, but I'll look tomorrow?"

"Beck sent a cryptic message specifically to Luc through one of the old back channels. It had something to do with strange things going on here. Rainey trusts us to investigate."

"Strange things going on here?" My eyes almost popped out. "Didn't I tell you that?"

"Calm down. All you have to be is the messenger-go-between."

"Am I going to do this on my own?"

"No, I'll stay close. In fact, I must talk to Rainey about a plan I doped out."

"I've never met Luc Raines, and I know you trust him, but doesn't this all sound crazy?"

"No. He's the real deal and this is a good case for us. If it gets really crazy, we're out!"

When I smiled, Pat put her arms around me and gave me a hug. I could smell her signature rose-petal perfume and realized how much I missed her company. Watching her shadow slip out the door, a twinge of envy came over me. No doubt, she was on her way to meet the handsome man who had lit up her smile. And while I wanted her to be happy, I understood that my twin in this life's adventures was stepping away from widowhood. Feeling left behind, I wondered if I would ever be able to take that step?

The following morning, Cheryl arrived after breakfast and shoved the wheelchair up against my bed ... again. "Let's go!" She tapped her wristwatch. "Tick, Tock!"

Sliding across the bed, I let out a snort. "How often do I have to go to upper therapy?"

"Five days a week. Today, a second therapist for your lower body gets you after me."

Climbing into the wheelchair, my hands pushed the rubber tires until I got through the door and around the corner. Cheryl was not behind me, but I kept pushing the wheels hard and fast along the corridor until I made it into the gym without her. The place was packed. Dutifully, my eyes spun around looking for that miracle worker ... Beck.

There he stood, tall and lean, working with an older man on a raised leather table. This old world spy looked younger than I had imagined sporting the same black polo and khaki pants as the other therapists. He must have felt my eyes boring into his back. He stopped massaging his patient's leg to turn around and search. His sad brown eyes found mine and locked on to me.

Cheryl distracted me. "Pull up to Darlene again. You two work well together."

Sliding next to Darlene's chair, she gave me a sly thumbs up. "Hey girlfriend, check it out!" Before I had a chance to ask more, Darlene eyed a tall three-piece-suit leaning against the wall. The handsome man stood taller than the group of everyday folks listening to him. His charisma and easy manner were in the style of Bill Clinton and he had the crowd in his pocket..

Darlene brought me back. "Looks like the Big Bad Wolfe is on tour duty today."

"Why is that man is so sexy?" I sighed. "And reminding me that I'm a woman."

"Ditto on that! Wilder Wolfe can do that to a gal." Darlene rolled her shoulders, pretending to shiver with excitement. "Makes me want to light up a cigarette."

We both laughed until Cheryl brought over our hand weights and began our upper body exercises. Working in unison to Cheryl's count, we pumped our arms up and down. Still, my eyes kept roaming across the room to look at the man's dimpled smile. He suddenly zeroed in on me and I froze unable to turn away. He stared into my eyes until his slow smile made me blush.

Trying to get into rhythm with Darlene's hand exercises, she gave me a knowing wink and we smiled at each other. Still, I felt Wilder Wolfe's eyes boring into my back. The sensation felt like wild fire running through my mind and body. It was as if I had plugged back in to the hot energy of life and I wondered when I had unplugged?

As the visitors left the gym, Wilder Wolfe leaned against the door frame saying goodbye. His presence unnerved me or maybe it was the drugs they had been feeding me.

When our session ended, Cheryl directed me to stay behind. Darlene wheeled over to the door and looked up at the director with her Cheshire smile. I watched as he bent down and gave her a big hug. Darlene turned and gave me a victory wave. Although I smiled back, I almost felt jealous and wondered what was causing my weird feelings?

. Cheryl brought me back to task. "Here comes your secondary therapist." She nodded to the blonde woman approaching. "Lulu will be working with you to keep your leg muscles from atrophy." That was when a bubble burst in my brain and I remembered that it was mandatory that I connect with Beck for my lower exercise program.

When Cheryl walked away, I was left with this petite blonde whose eyes twinkled like stars. Her smile grew as she told me how eager she was to help me get back on my feet. I went blank. What could I do? I had to get Beck into this position without hurting Lulu's feelings?

Dozens of schemes crossed my mind as she spoke so lovingly with a slight Russian accent. "Although you are not weight bearing, we will get you up on the parallel bars and you will be able to hop on your good leg. You need to be standing straight so the blood can flow freely. That will be our goal." She stopped to catch her breath and hear me agree.

And that is when I let her have it. "What the hell are you talking about?"

Lulu's sweet face dropped to the floor. "I'm only trying to help you stay strong."

"You're crazy. Do you know that? My doctor doesn't want me up on my feet."

She looked confused. "I can call him to make sure." Poor woman was still trying to placate me. When she turned to go make the phone call, I spun my wheelchair out the door and up the corridor. Racing back to my room, I crawled into bed and waited for the ugly scene.

Within minutes, Lulu walked into my room wearing a smile. "Ms. Hennessey, your doctor reassured me that you could stand and hop, hold onto bars. He encourages this activity. Don't worry about falling. I will put this strap around your waist. Please, let's try?"

Without looking at her, I went into my sinister act. "I don't want to work with you. Your voice bothers me and we will never get along. Besides, I heard that Beck's an excellent physical therapist ... much better than you. I will only work with him."

Out of the corner of my eye I saw her shoulders droop. Lulu threw up her hands and looked sad. "Okay, I'm done here." She turned on her heel and walked out the door.

I wanted to call after her ... tell her that I was sorry ... tell her that I had a job to do.

Chapter Six

I was eating the last of my dinner while watching the birds take their sunset flight. Chasing their last meal of the day, they zoomed across the mosquitoes hovering above the river water below.   Mr. Sanderson was cooing to Margaret as he sliced her meat and I almost felt jealous. Ernie was the kind of male who could delicately launder lingerie and still maintain his manhood. No wonder Margaret had hot dreams about her eighty-something husband.

My serenity ended as an elderly lady in a black dress walked past the divider curtain and entered my part of the room. Her grey hair tied in a bun, granny glasses and nun shoes did not match her smooth skin. Looking closer, I spotted Pat's twinkling eyes.

Happy to see her in the daylight I whispered, "Why the spinster getup?"

She spun around to show her entire transformation. "I put myself down as your Aunt Frieda in the guest book."

"Aunt Frieda never looked so good. But again, why are you incognito?"

"Trying to avoid being caught on security photos."

"Is there heavy surveillance here?"

"Across the Potomac from the Capitol? You bet. Leaving Georgetown Pike, motion sensors pick up all movement. Cameras follow everyone in the public sectors of the buildings."

"Inside the rooms, too?"

"Unknown? There are rules about privacy. If they have cameras in the rooms, they're well hidden." She took off her glasses and sat on the commode. Looking closely at me, she looked worried. "You don't look so good. How're you doing?"

"I did a dirty trick on a nice therapist today. She was ready to work with me and I screamed at her to go away because I preferred Beck." Tears of remorse filled my eyes. "I feel awful! The poor woman ran out the door and I'll never forget the hurt look on her face."

Pat leaned forward and patted my hand as her other hand snuck the chocolate chip cookie off my tray. "Therapists get hollered at all the time. She's used to it. I wouldn't worry." The cookie went into Pat's mouth in one piece and I heard her teeth grinding it up. "Good cookie!"

"Yeah, I was told we only get a cookie once a week."

"Awe, and today's the day?" .

I let her say she was sorry until I could no longer hold back my snicker. Her old lady face switched from sad to mad. "You are an awful friend! Making me feel bad." We both laughed until we heard Mr. Sanderson pushing Margaret out the door for their evening trip to the patio.

"Let's get serious. What's new with," I brought up my hand and coughed out, "Raines?"

"I met him for a late night supper at The Willard last night." She smiled coyly.

"Tell me it was for business?" My voice sounded harsh.

Her eyes swirled and looked dreamy. "Luc's going to give us a lotta business."

"Pat, do we have paperwork for this job?"

"I'm working on it. Rainey says this is a special job that cannot go through channels."

"Oh crap! We're working for free?"

"No, he gave me an advance of five grand."

"Company check or cash?"

"Cash, but he says he's doing us a favor. He wants us to have running money while you are in here to keep the business going. Nice of him, don't you think?" Her face wrinkled up in a sweet smile that I knew so well. It was the smile that she used to get me to agree to anything.

"Pat, you know the drill! Cash means this job is either a personal request of Luc Raines or we're working a Black Op for the agency. Either one scares the hell out of me as I lay helpless in this bed."

"Oh Meg, you worry too much. Don't over dramatize this deal. Let's look at the goody bag I brought you the other night." Pat pulled out the large black duffel bag from the wardrobe. "Luc is so thoughtful, he threw in most of these things for you." She pulled out a strange looking cell phone and handed it to me. "This is a SAT phone. It's clean and does not have the normal GPS chip. Totally untraceable through cell sites because it signals to their satellite. He gave me one too."

"You mean now he can call you and me and track our whereabouts?"

"Well yeah, but he is our client. Only natural that he'll want to reach out sometimes." She changed the subject by pulling out a big flashlight. When she turned it on, the beam of light was amazingly bright. Pat giggled, "For Henny to see what's hiding in the dark corners."

"That's not funny, partner. You forget, I can't run."

She showed me a dark jogging suit. "So you can crawl around at night." We both laughed at that crazy thought as she put everything back. "Look Meg, there's a phony bottom. Below are some trade tools I felt you might need. Check them out when you feel up to it." She put the bag away and pulled out a small package from her purse. "Here's a store bought cell phone that I loaded with your family's numbers. Too bad they all live out of town and can't visit."

"Thanks, I still wonder what happened to mine. Must've lost it when I fell."

"Was it on a contract?"

"No. I bought minutes with my credit card."

Pat smiled. "Let's call and see if anyone answers." She dialed my old number on the new phone in her hand and we listened to it ring over the speaker. Three rings and my recorded voice came on, saying the usual please-leave-a-number message.

"I should probably shut down that number since the phone is lost to me."

"No. Keep it on and let's see what happens."

The voice coming over the ceiling speakers announced that visiting hours were over. Pat got up to leave. "I'll be interested to hear what Beck has to say tomorrow. Make good mental notes." When I nodded, she waved goodbye and pretended to hobble out of the room.

I fell asleep watching the news and felt my dreaming self float above the bed and out the window. Drifting past the cliff and above the river rushing below, it became my dream's desire to visit my young husband and baby son. As always, I felt exhilarated to travel back in time to that house where we all lived happily, but not ever after.

Daylight brought me back to my real world where my mornings were becoming routine. Mary and Lyric assisted me to wash up, eat breakfast and get dressed while in bed. The immobilizer kept my right leg perfectly straight while it recovered. The rest of me was trying to recover from the trauma of the fall and being prisoner at Barrington Hall.

As usual, Cheryl came banging into the room with the chair. I was ready for her and jumped inside it. Out the door, I rumbled up the hallway. Speeding along, I spotted Darlene slow rolling ahead of me. I whizzed past her and yelled out, "Beat you to the door!"

The race was on. She took my challenge and pounded her rubber wheels to catch up. When I heard her smoky laughter next to me, I pushed even harder. Neck and neck, we hit the gym entrance together. Laughing and gasping for air, we found an audience of patients who usually looked sleepy. Catching our fun, they cheered and clapped as we flew past the door.

"That's enough play time!" Cheryl screeched from behind. "Go park against the wall. You two girls need to do more reps since you have so much energy this morning." Darlene and I cursed under our breaths, but parked our chairs and waited for our hand weights.

At the end of Cheryl's session, Beck came over and pushed my chair to the leather table without a word. I got myself out of the chair hopping on one leg and moving by myself to lay on the table. His look was stern. "Who taught you to transport that way?"

"I taught myself and it works for me."

"You think you're smart, huh?"

Searching his eyes, I saw that he was not kidding. Beck's sad outside personae did not do justice to the strict inner code of the man. My sense was that he had led a lean life without excess and would not be the first Eastern European who scorned the soft American lifestyle.

I did not want to be caught in a power struggle with him and changed my tactic. "Independent girl, but I'm smart enough to know when to listen." That brought out his smile.

"Good Meg, because we are going to do hard work to keep your leg alive."

"I'm ready. Whatever you say, Beck!"

He began by making me raise both legs in a variety of positions still wearing the heavy brace. The muscles in my right leg began to twitch, but I did not complain and accomplished everything Beck demanded in his low voice. And once I showed that I could accomplish this feat, he made me do it over and over and over again. As the crowd in the gym thinned out to go to their rooms or the cafeteria for lunch, my task master continued. I exercised until after noon, wondering when the hell this session was going to stop. I needed pain meds and I needed a nap.

Sweating from exhaustion after two grueling hours, I was ready to call a halt when Beck whispered softly. "I hear there's strange comings and goings in the basement late at night."

I had almost forgot why I was on Beck's table. "Who told you this?"

"The workers talk." He lifted his shoulders. "I listen."

"Can you go down and check it out."

"No. The therapists here are contract workers and leave in the afternoon. Only employees are allowed to move about the building."

"What do you want me to do?"

"Tell Luc, I heard the name of his old enemy."

"Why can't you tell him yourself?"

"Luc does not want to be connected with me and ... vice versa."

"What's the message you want me to pass along?"

"Tell Luc that Mortez has a presence here ... somehow, someway. Tell him I'm worried."

Chapter Seven

After my strenuous workout and hearing Beck's small piece of information, I was left physically spent and mentally unsatisfied. Trying to ponder the significance of Beck's message, was no use. My focus kept wandering to the window to enjoy the last of the brilliant pink sky. When I did try to analyze this investigation Pat had gotten us into, it seemed too easy. I almost felt guilty about the five Gs Pat had collected from Raines. Still, our new business had taken in six thousand this month. Add that to the fifty grand we had donated from our own bank accounts to use as startup funds and we were on our way to an office: Hannelly & Hennessey Investigations.

Hours later, long after dark, I woke up to hands shaking me out of a dreamless sleep. "Hey sleepy girl, wake up." Pat smiled down and held out an open bag of cheese popcorn. It smelled so good that I sat up and took a handful. We both tossed orange kernels into our mouths and made yummy sounds before I gave her an update.

Pat opened two colas and listened patiently. When I fed her the few lines that Beck had passed to me, she wrinkled up her nose. "That's it?" My nod was her answer. "Sounds like scrawny intel, if you ask me?"

"Not worth the money we were paid to retrieve it. That's for sure."

"How about that odd name ... *Mortez*? I'll run it on the Web. See if I get any hits."

Her plan frightened me. "Back away from that idea. Every agency looking down at the Net will want to know why you have an interest." I warned. "We have to trust Raines on this."

"You're right. I don't need anyone looking back at me."

"You know the policy." I laughed. "Why do you have an interest in this man?"

Pat sighed. "Maybe Rainey will tell me more."

"Beck never gave me a clear reason why he felt there were strange things going on in the basement either. It felt as if he might be putting out a teaser?"

"I'll pass that along when I see Luc tonight."

"Another midnight supper?" My tone may have sounded snide.

"Yeah, but not at the Willard. Tonight we meet at the Mayflower."

"Pat, please tell me you're not crossing the customer/contractor line with him?"

"Never. This is strictly business, besides his two henchmen always hang in the background. Rainey keeps it all business. Says he's excited to work with our little female operation and he pays the highest regard to our husbands."

"If it ever got out that your relationship with Raines was personal? The ladies working at Langley would spit on our names. We'd never get work from them again. You do understand?"

"Hey, all those babes wish they could sleep with him." She laughed. "Don't worry, our partnership means more than a tryst with a sexy man." Her smile was not reassuring.

As soon as Pat left, my head fell back on the pillow. Deep in a nonsensical dream, I enjoyed my slumber until I perceived movement. Opening my eyes slowly, I tried to linger in the last remnants of sleep until I saw a shadow entering my side of the curtain. Safety alarms began going off in the back of my head. Before screaming, I tried to formulate a question to ask the man fast approaching the side of my bed.

Before I had time for niceties, his hands reached out and began to pull down my covers. I felt the cold night air waft across my exposed hips and legs. Frightened, I reached down to stop his large hand from moving across my naked belly. Somehow in my delirium I mumbled, "What're you doing?"

A tiny spot of light swept across my eyes. It was blue bright and it blinded me. Waiting for his answer, I only heard a coarse voice demand, "Diaper check!"

Rubbing my eyes, I could only see his shadow looming over my bed. "I don't wear diapers!" The light in my eyes went off, but I could not see. Finding the call button, I pressed it.

Within seconds, the CNA on duty rushed thru the door. Before coming to my bed, she turned off the call light flashing red on the wall. "What's the matter?" She asked softly.

"A man was in here pulling down my covers. Said he was doing a *diaper check*?"

"A man? Hmmm, we're an all-girl shift tonight. Did you recognize him?"

"No, I just felt the hair on the back of his hand."

"Hair on his hand? Wasn't he wearing gloves?"

The next three days went by slowly. Both Cheryl and Beck worked the muscles in my body until tears ran from my eyes. Pat had been a no-show since we ate popcorn and I wondered what she was up to these past days ... and nights. I called both my son and two sisters to give them a mumbo-jumbo story as to how I fell in Georgetown at four a.m. All three wanted to travel to Virginia, but I convinced them that I was healing nicely with no time, nor desire, to visit.

My only diversion from the rigors of this place was Darlene. She had invited me out to the patio every afternoon until it became routine. Sitting outside was refreshing. The flora and fauna grew wild along the high cliffs where they enjoyed the rising mist from the river below.

Darlene turned out to be a natural story teller. Cigarette in hand, her little vignettes revealed every facet of her life. She described the building that she owned in Arlington; her tavern was below and her living quarters were above. After a few days of me showing enjoyment for her outrageous bar stories, she began to let me in on her secrets.

I looked shocked when Darlene whispered that it was not an accident that had brought her to Barrington Hall. "It was that son-of-a-bitch, *Harold.* We were fighting like alley cats up in the flat. The bastard could not stop dicking around with the bar bitches!"

I winced just enough that she understood how I felt her pain.

"That night I had had it with that man. I stood on the landing, throwing his crap down the stairs. He heard me screaming, even in the tavern, and came running up the steps after me." She stopped to chuckle at the picture now playing out in her mind. "I ran like hell to the apartment, but he caught me at the door and yanked out a fistful of my hair." She pointed to a prominent bald spot. "That bull of a man is strong. He picked me up and threw my fat ass down the staircase." She took a long drag off her cigarette, but did not put it out. "Can you believe that?"

I nodded, realizing how Darlene had lost those teeth."Geez Darlene, is he locked up?"

Her soulful eyes looked down. "Nah! When the cops showed up from our shouting at each other, I lied. Couldn't see putting the poor guy in jail." She lit a new cigarette with the butt of her old one and shook her head. "Anyway, he's got asthma."

"What about when you get out of here?"

"I'll get my sons to kick his sorry ass out of the flat before I go home."

As I mixed and mingled with the patients and staff, I kept a vigilant eye for my night intruder. Although I was never told officially that the man who came into my room was not supposed to be there, I knew it to be true. Whoever it was had knowledge of the facility in order to freely roam the place in the night.

All kinds of workmen walked the halls during the day, repairing and installing. Any one of them could figure out how to gain entrance to the complex. My guess was that the man in my room was an everyday pervert and the rehab patients, who took sleeping pills every night, were easy prey. Still, I wondered whether that same pervert was employed by the facility?

Pat finally showed up late in the day at the end of the week. Wearing the same light blue scrubs as Mary and Lyrie, I did not recognize her at first. She fooled me again and I was curious. "Why do you look like the CNAs?"

"Because I now work here on the evening shift. What do you think of that?"

"Since when are you a CNA?"

"You forgot. I got certified when my mother was diagnosed stage four breast cancer. She wanted to die at home and the training came in handy when Neal became ill. Besides, Rainey arranged for my paperwork and recommendations. This way, I get to keep an eye on you."

"I don't buy it. Tell me the real reason you're here?"

"What I said is true, but Luc gave me new instructions."

"No, no more instructions from Luc." I put up my hands to try and stop her. "There's something way off at this place. I can't quite explain it, but I want to get out of here." Seeing Pat's eyes widen, I realized how crazy I must've appeared.

She softened, "Forgive me. You've been under a lot of strain. I'll take care of everything. You rest." She kissed my cheek and I watched her pony tail sway as she walked out the door.

Chapter Eight

Dr. Saville stood tall, dark and handsome with his back to me while reading the films his nurse had just taken of my knee. "X-rays look good, kiddo. The cap's staying in place." He turned away from the light box and winked. "You've been a good girl, staying off your leg these past weeks." His smile dropped. "I hate to tell you this, but you've got a few more left to go."

As I sat in my wheelchair smiling into his pale blue eyes, my face froze when he made the pronouncement for more time in rehab. The subject had to be changed or I would have cried. "In my next life? I'm coming back as a man," My statement came out of left field, but he was kind and laughed along with me.

"I mean it, Doc. Look at you. You're supremely happy. Let me guess." My eyes drifted along the office walls. His university and hospital certifications heralded his mastering the science of medicine, orthopedics and surgery. Then there were the pictures of his lovely wife and smiling children. "I can see that you have a great life."

"Funny you should bring up that subject." His eyes twinkled. "We were just talking about reincarnation here in the office, today. And I did say that this life's been damn good to me."

"I rest my case." I should not have been comparing his life to mine.

The good doctor stayed quiet, making notes on my chart that had rode along me from Barrington. Every once in awhile, Dr. Saville stopped to take a long look at me before returning to his remarks. Without looking up he asked, "You seem a little blue today. How're you feeling?"

"I don't want to go back to Barrington Hall. That's how I'm feeling." When he rushed to suggest another facility, I told the truth. "No. The place's okay. They treat me fine. I'm just sick of being confined. I hate to be locked up and I feel like I'm doing time!"

He kept writing on my chart and actually sped up to jot down even more. "Tell you what, since you're such a good patient, I'll tell your therapist to take off your Immobilizer and begin electrical stimulation. That'll work to strengthen your leg muscles and step up your progress." He must have seen my face soften. "Don't get cocky now. Still no weight on that knee, or we'll both be crying as they wheel you back in surgery."

During the return ride in the medivan, my wheel chair swayed behind my young Barrington Hall attendant who had come with me. She chatted amiably with the young driver, but I did not listen closely until they discussed the many break-ins at medical facilities. They agreed that gangs were looking to steal drugs.

Wheeling myself into my room, I saw the Sanderson family hovering around Margaret dressed in street clothes. Her suitcases sat next to her wheelchair. She smiled, "Today's the day."

Tears welled in my eyes. "Oh Margaret, I forgot you're going home. I'll miss you." And, I meant it. "Take care and don't come back." The frail lady blew a kiss off the tip of her fingers as she was pushed past me. An empty silence filled room 112.

Transferring my body from the wheelchair onto the bed was never an easy task. My bag of bones suddenly weighed a ton and my heart was not in the challenge. I felt sad and alone. Sick of being in bed, I pushed a pillow over my face. Nagging grief and the need to stay there for more weeks overtook me. Sorry for myself, I blubbered until I felt hands rubbing my shoulders.

Throwing off the pillow, I saw the worried faces of my favorite CNAs, Mary and Lyrie. They reassured me until Angela came running into the room, holding out pain meds and a paper cup of water. After swallowing the pills, I smiled at these three wonderful women who had become my advocates without me realizing it.

Mary spoke up, "Don't worry. We'll help you get through this."

At midnight that night, Pat waltzed in wearing a smile and showing her usual energy. "This CNA job's not so bad. I'm working calls from your end of the hall. So far, the floor's been quiet and the staff's playing cards in the gym." She sat down on my commode and took a closer look at me. "They got you on the Watch List for depression. Nice work, Henny. They won't be assigning a new patient for this room. You'll have the place all to yourself. How'd you do that?"

"I traveled to the surgeon's office today. I must've looked depressed to him."

"Smart thinking! What gave you that brilliant idea?"

"Don't give me credit. The bone doc ordered weeks more of rehab and I got sick to my stomach. He wrote copious notes on my chart and when I got back here, I enjoyed a crying jag. It was probably the combination that put me on the Watch List."

"It worked out well. We'll have time to explore and find out what's going on here."

"Don't tell me this case is still active?"

"Yes, and we got another five grand. Rainey is very interested in Beck's information.

"Why would Luc Raines pay attention to that flimsy message?"

"Here's the heads-up straight from Luc's mouth. Long after the end of the Cold War, old spies and young agents of all stripes were being tracked, stalked and assassinated."

"The Russians?"

"Both the U.S. and Russia denied culpability along with the dismantled East German Stasi and Israel's stealth Mossad. The world intelligence community came to the realization that an unaffiliated rogue was practicing his craft or showing off his skills."

"These events never went public?"

"No. Every operative on the globe was briefed on the carnage and told to stay alert or die.

"There was no other information about the killer?"

"That strange name, *Mortez*, was left behind to mark the trophy kills.

"There was a serial killer stalking intelligence agents?"

"That's the way every smart mind saw it. Luc says getting this guy is still a top priority even though there's not been a killing of an intel officer for years now."

I scratched my head. "Hard to believe. With all the high tech spy equipment ... even back then, you'd think they'd have found this guy?"

Chapter Nine

Pat and I devised our plan of operation: I would stay connected to Beck, but not reveal that my partner was working there. We would keep that detail quiet along with how I was relaying information back to Raines. My duty was to keep the lines of communication open with Beck and gather daytime information while Pat poked around during the nighttime.

The next day in therapy, Darlene and I parked next to each other as usual. When we began to go through our upper body routine, we could not help but act silly. We made funny faces every time Cheryl turned her back. Worse, we upped the repetition count so many times when she was not paying attention that the two of us could not keep the numbers straight.

Out of the corner of my eye, I spotted LuLu standing back with her arms folded. There was a frown on her face as she glared at our antics. Rubbing her right index finger across her left, she sent the shame-on-you message to us which made me feel ashamed ... again.

Darlene could not see LuLu, but she saw my playful mood melt. "What's wrong?"

"LuLu caught us making fun of Cheryl behind her back."

Darlene ignored this revelation while never missing a beat with her hand exercises. "Who's LuLu to mock us? I always see her whispering in Beck's ear. I figure she's either complaining how bad all of us smell. Or, she's flirting with Beck."

My ears perked up. "She could have a thing for him. How does he react?"

"He takes it all in, but never seems to respond in a sensual way. Know what I mean?"

I nodded. "Maybe, he doesn't care for Russian woman. He did grow up in Poland?"

Darlene laughed, "In today's market? Could be he doesn't care for women ... period!"

When it came time for me to work the muscles in my legs, Beck grabbed my chart and studied Dr. Saville's notes. As I pulled myself from the wheelchair to Beck's workout table, I saw his eyes light up as they rolled across the good doctor's instructions.

He looked up and saw me ready to exercise. "Good, Meg, we can remove your immobilizer for massage and stimulation. Innocent electrical currents applied to the front of your thigh will remind your quads they are strongest muscles," he smiled, "I am excited!"

As we worked through the new routine, I secretly kept an eye on LuLu as she secretly kept an eye on Beck. Seeing her sneak peeks at him, when she thought no one was looking, did make me feel that quite possibly she had an attraction for him. Darlene was probably right. Still, I knew that all intelligence gatherers utilized emotion to gain information. I had no doubt that Beck, coming out of the dark world of the Soviet Union, was also capable of flirting with the Russian woman if for no other reason than to expand his little spy network at Barrington Hall.

Looking around the gym at the other therapists, a real world fact hit me. Many of them had immigrated from foreign lands that only a few decades ago were considered enemies of the United States. Now, these citizens live and move freely around our country.

"Time to hook you up." Beck interrupted my thoughts and began placing sticky rubber circles to areas around my knee. Once his hands pulled the wires back to a black box, he turned the dial and I jumped. The odd sensation felt as if tiny bugs were inside my flesh. It took me a few gulps of air to calm down and accept the electricity swirling in and around my knee.

When Beck saw my reaction, he bent down and looked sincere. "Can you tolerate this?"

"I'm fine, really." And while I had him close added, "Do you have more information?"

Beck turned to adjust the machine when a female voice screamed out. It sounded like an awkward version of ... *HELP!*

We looked to see an elderly woman bouncing around in a wheelchair across the gym. Eyes rolling, arms flailing, lips quivering ... she appeared to be in pain. Huffing and puffing, she tried to form a word, but all that came out was her eerie cry for help.

"That's Genevieve," Beck looked back at me, "she's usually docile and never talks." We watched as two therapists ran to Genevieve's side and consoled her. Beck used the diversion to whisper, "I spotted another delivery to Base A ... the old gym downstairs. The package arrived via a private trucking company. The shipper was *Mortez & Associates*."

"Can't you get down there to check it out?"

"I would have no reason to leave this floor. The space downstairs is locked and not being used except for storage. Cameras are all over down there."

Here was my chance to ask, "Are there cameras hidden inside the patients' rooms?"

Beck shrugged. "Patient privacy would suggest not, but I would not trust it."

"How much security is there here?"

"Two guards are standard. One's usually mobile. The other watches the monitors in their office downstairs next to the Director."

"How can I get my hands on that door key to the old gym?"

"Copies of all keys are locked up at every Nurses' Station for all three floors."

"Do you have anything else to relay to Raines?"

"Yes, tell Luc I appreciate the deposit."

"Will do. Now, let's get this e-stim over with," I smiled, "I'm hungry."

Late in the night, I hit the call button and Pat came running. "Hey Meg, how are you?" Before I could answer, she ran to turn off the light flashing on the wall. "Geez, we're having trouble with Genevieve tonight. I heard the old gal is usually so sweet, but tonight she won't quiet down. She's not in pain. Can't figure out why she keeps calling out?"

"She can't tell you what's wrong?"

"No, she suffered a stroke a while back and isn't able to speak."

"She kept hollering out when they brought her into the gym today. I sensed she's scared."

"The poor dear has no relatives. It's so sad. Let's change the subject. How are you?"

"I'm back on the job."

"I never knew you were off." She laughed heartily. "You know our slogan?"

"We have a slogan?" I laughed with her.

Pat pretended to be serious and started a little sing-song. "Hannelly and Hennessey, we're never off the job. Come rain or shine? Slip and fall? Sustain a broken knee cap? We'll find a way to keep on the job!" She burst out laughing and how could I not laugh with her even though it was at my expense.

When we stopped laughing she asked, "Did you talk to Beck?"

"Beck has spotted at least one box from a no-name delivery service."

Pat crinkled up her nose. "What's so odd about that?"

"It was addressed for delivery to Base A, the old gym not being utilized."

"I've wanted to get downstairs and check out that place."

"Here's the topper. The return address was *Mortez & Associates*."

"That's the strange name we keep hearing. Did you ask Beck about securing access?"

"He said duplicate keys are locked up at each Nurse's Station. Be careful of the cameras."

"Spotted a few in the hallways already." Pat added.

"Beck didn't know if there are any in the patient quarters."

"I doubt it, but let's check out this room for pinpoint lenses and listening devices." Pat moved around while chattering about the hot days of summer and what the President was doing.

Watching her strong hands probe for monitoring equipment, I had to smile. "Neal sure taught you a lot about spy equipment."

She kept pulling out drawers and checking the bottoms. After crawling out from under both beds, she dusted off her scrubs and spoke into my ear. "I'm not able to pull apart the overhead lights or televisions. But, I would suggest that you consider yourself under a listening surveillance until we know for sure." She fluffed my pillow and straightened my sheets.

I teased her, "You're such a good little CNA."

"Ah, you tell that to all the girls and boys who wear the uniform."

I whispered, "Beck is grateful for the deposit. Tell Raines."

HIDING PLACES AT BARRINGTON HALL

Chapter Ten

During the following week, both Cheryl and Beck explained how I needed to perform additional exercise in order to restore my muscle strength. How could I argue? The weeks in bed had taken their toll. After having a pep talk with myself, I resolved to get the muscles working again. My plan was to get additional workouts designed by both upper and lower therapists and perform them in the early evenings when the gym was empty.

I had to admit that it was fun wheeling around after dinner and it was delightful to have the gym all to myself. These added routines were advantageous for another reason. The afternoon shift, busy with dinner and showers, got used to my roaming the halls and not always being in my room. My new freedom allowed me to scoot past people without notice.

One evening not long after, Darlene rolled into the gym holding up a cigarette: her signal to join her outside. I took a double take. She did not look herself. Instead of her sly smile promising funny stories, I caught apprehension on her face.

We wheeled in tandem to the patio, where we sat and watched rolling shades of red and orange cross the sky. Since this was her show, I sucked in my breath and waited.

She lit up and let out her first puff. "Harold told my kids he's gonna kill me."

"Oh no! That's not good, Darlene. You don't think he means it?"

"He never means it when he's been drinking. Cold sober? Yeah, he's a man of his word."

"What're you going to do?"

Darlene pulled out a silver switchblade and handed it to me. It was long with a pearl handle. It felt smooth, but cold to the touch. Fear gripped me in the gut and I began to worry about Darlene's safety. "Do you think you'll need this?"

Busy relighting her cigarette, she took her second long drag and let the cloud of smoke swirl in and out of her mouth. "Can't trust the son-of-a-bitch!"

Noticing my finger print smudges left behind on Darlene's blade, I quickly rubbed the silver against my tee. When she looked at me and took notice of my frenzy I explained, "I apologize. My hands are full of sweat."

A second later, her eyes were no longer looking at me. They were squinting at the building behind me. When my head turned to look back at our domicile, I spotted that same older woman, Genevieve. She was standing at her window, eyes bulging and mouth wide open. I could not look away from her and then it happened. A dark shadow of a man came up from behind and wrapped his arms around her throat. Genevieve disappeared.

As I turned to Darlene, her wheelchair was already speeding to the building entrance. I pulled up behind her and hit the handicap button. When the doors opened, we both spun our wheels around the cafeteria tables and chairs to reach the hallway. Flying past the Nurse's Station, Darlene hollered out to the lone white uniform. "Attack! Attack! Follow us."

The nurse dropped her chart, tripped down the three steps to run around the counter. All three of us headed for Genevieve's room, but Darlene was the first in the door. The old woman was sitting up in bed, alone. Wide-eyed and looking scared, her mouth kept making a perfect circle like a fish, but no sound came out. The nurse ran to her side while Darlene and I searched with our eyes. There was no one else in the room.

When the nurse was able to calm the poor woman, Darlene and I left. She led me back to the patio. "Now, I really need a smoke."

I yelled back, "I could use a drink!"

When we were outside again I asked, "What the hell do you think we saw?"

She took a long puff off her cigarette. "There *was* a man in that room."

"And I think he was up to no good." I wiped the sweat off my brow.

"Poor ole gal can't talk." Darlene shook her head and took another drag. "I think he's tormenting Genevieve. And I'd bet he's the reason why she's screaming all the time?"

Chapter Eleven

I left Darlene after we wheeled through the dark cafeteria. She took off left down the corridor and I turned right. As I rolled past Genevieve's room, I looked inside. The soft bed light bathed across her face and, except for her eyes being wide open, she looked like a corpse. I slowed to take a closer look. She never turned her head, but her eyes stayed wide open ... watching.

Pat came running up from behind with a clipboard in her hand. She followed me into my room and asked, "Hey, the bosses want your statement about what went on this evening?" I must have made an inquisitive look because she added, "The Nurse's Station called the Assistant Director. "He ordered a quiet investigation to avoid outside trouble." She plopped down on the closed commode, pulled out a pen and readied herself to record my remarks on a very official looking form.

"What does that mean ... outside trouble?" Her tone was beginning to aggravate me.

"Everyone fears that the county, or even the Commonwealth, will come marching in and demand an inspection because of the rumors there's abuse when it's really patient hallucination."

I turned cold. "Don't tell me you've gone over to management's side already?"

"What're you talking about? I just want you to tell me what happened?"

"It wasn't just me, Darlene saw it too. And remember, I told you there was something odd about that sweet lady. She can't stop screaming."

Pat sighed so hard her bangs flew up. "Whaddaya want me to write down on this report?"

"How come management isn't here anxious to find out firsthand what happened?"

"The CNA is your first line of defense and management refrains from crossing that line."

Now I sighed to blow off steam. "Management is not the enemy, or is it?"

Pat jumped up from the commode and hugged me. "You've been here too long."

"No, that's not right. I could turn around and say ... you don't want to fight the system."

"Put yourself in management's position. It's only fair that they question you and Darlene away from their influence." She made one of her funny faces that always got a smile out of me. I gave her a slow on as I thought about it. Patricia Hannelly always showed great logic.

"Let's get the details on paper." She sat down again and positioned herself to write.

I took myself back to that moment. "It was getting dark, but the sky was still on fire. There was still plenty of light for us to see each other. Since my back was to the building, it was Darlene who caught sight of Genevieve in her window. Following Darlene's eyes, I turned and saw poor Genevieve up against the window with her mouth open. It was hard to hear her screams, but I did. Within seconds, an unknown male pulled her back into the dark room."

"How'd you know it was a male?"

"There was something tall and muscular about the shadow."

"Hey, your eyes are not that sharp. Do you think Darlene may have got a better look?"

"Maybe? Can you go and ask her?"

"Her CNA will get her report." She looked up at me. "For now, lay low. Stay out of this ... whatever it is. We've got our own work to do here."

"You're right. Anything new on your end?"

"Yes, I've checked out the basement to see what lives down there. The administration offices, security, laundry and main kitchen take up most of the square footage. A little beauty shop and Base A, which is the old gym occupy the rest of it."

"Did you get into the old gym?"

"No, I have not been able to get my hands on a key. Here's my plan. Although you are still not allowed to take a shower, you can be wheeled downstairs to get your hair shampooed. I'll snatch both door keys from the Nurse's Station. How does that sound?"

"That sounds heavenly. I've been trying to bend over my little sink, but it doesn't work."

"Good. I have us scheduled to go down late tomorrow night. Be ready at ten." She opened the wardrobe and pulled out the duffel bag. Pat dug past the first layer full of toiletries. "I can't remember what I stuffed in here." She brought out a penlight and handed it to me. "This will come in handy."

Her smile dropped as she showed me that cell phone again. "Don't forget this phone's got an added battery pack if you ever need connectivity." She stopped to catch her breath, but I knew Pat was bracing herself to reveal information that I might not take well. "Don't be surprised if you get an unexpected call on this phone. Keep it handy."

Pat wanted to roll on, but I put up my hand. "By unexpected call, you mean Luc Raines?"

"Exactly." The set of her face begged that I trust her on this and I acquiesced.

Her final retrievals were a can of pepper spray labeled hair spray and a nail file. "You can keep these in plain sight."

I felt the file's fine point. "Did you sharpen this?"

She grinned, "Love the tools on Neal's workbench."

Looking at my pitiful weapons of defense I had to admit, "Wish I had my .22 with me."

"No can do! There's one area they canvas covertly here and that's your stuff. Those sweet gals who come for your laundry everyday are trained to search through your things with or without you in the room. They'll confiscate anything that might be deemed dangerous."

"What? They don't speak English and act so nice when they label our clothes."

"Yep they do all that, but they do speak English and that's their cover so you do not pay attention as they nose around."

I must have looked shocked, but changed the subject. "How goes your late suppers?"

"Haven't seen Luc since last time. I'm supposing that he's out of the country."

Chapter Twelve

The following day Darlene and I were working on our upper-body routine when she asked, "What did you say on the management report concerning Genevieve?"

Without hesitation I said, "The truth as we saw it."

"Good. And I plan to keep my eye on that poor woman." Darlene's fierce look of determination proved to me that she meant it. "Hey, since the females around here love whispering tidbits of gossip to Beck, find out if he's heard any strange things going on around Genevieve." I nodded as we completed the last of our hand-weight repetitions.

Waving goodbye to Darlene, I pushed the rubber wheels to the workout tables and waited for Beck. I sat and watched the therapists' activity as they ended one session and started another. LuLu caught my eye as she pushed an elderly woman, who I did not recognize, into the gym. The poor lady's head hung to the side, almost touching her shoulder. Even stranger looking, her head was covered with a nun's white wimple. The religious bonnet looked out of place with her grey sweat shirt and pants. Her eyes were glazed over and she stared out in wonderment.

When it came time for me to get up on the workout table, I asked Beck about the holy woman, now parked next to the broken-boned biker guy.

"That's Sister Elizabeth ... very sad," Beck dropped his eyes, "spinal degeneration."

I felt compelled to ask, "Can she speak?"

"She rambles mostly about the spirit world, angels and demons, that she sees roaming around. Her bone loss is traveling up her spine, weakening the neck. It's difficult for her to elevate her head or hold it up." Hearing her difficulties, I felt a chill and suddenly worried about this new woman's safety.

Beck began our routine and, since no one was paying attention to us, I questioned him about Genevieve. "I know she cannot communicate, but don't you think that sweet woman is acting strange ... always screaming as if she needs help?"

"I am well used to people screaming and acting strange. You came here from the wide-awake world where healthy people behave in a sane manner. It's not like that here. The elderly are losing their body strength, their bones are weakening. They're having little strokes ... not enough to paralyze, but enough to cause tiny damages to their thinking or body control."

"You're right." I sighed, "Back to business, do you have more intel to pass along?"

He rotated my good leg to keep those muscles from atrophy. "LuLu needed something yesterday out of storage in the old gym. When she tried to get the key at the First Floor Nurse's Station, the duty nurse said it had been taken away by management with no explanation."

"That is strange."

An hour later, when I called Pat on the cell she purchased to replace my missing one, an she reacted the same way and asked, "How in the hell will we be able to get in there tonight?" I could almost hear the wheels of her mind turning and stayed quiet to let her think. "There has to be copies in both the Director's Office and Security. Is there any way you could get down to the basement this afternoon and look around?"

Later that day, while the staff was busy cleaning up after the midday meal, I wheeled onto one of the two elevators and hit the down-button. When the doors opened one floor below, I was surprised to see so much activity. A multitude of people were traveling the corridors. Staff and visitors were going in and out of the main kitchen, lining up at the Beauty Shop and browsing inside the Gift Store.

It was my 'need for a cola' that got me past the eagle-eyed nurses always keeping an eye on us. I made a mental note to have a can of soda on my lap as I returned to the first floor.

Pushing along the basement hallways, I found where both the Security and Director's Offices were located. They stood side-by-side and both doors were swung open. Slowing down, I looked inside. Director Wolfe's secretary sat at the front desk filing her nails, but the door to his office was closed.

Next door, a uniformed guard talked on the phone. His conversation sounded personal, but his shrewd eyes never stopped scanning the wall of monitors directly across from him. Since he was alone, I assumed that his partner was out on patrol.

I pushed past the open door, past eye shot of the guard, but backed up a step to scrutinize their surveillance screens. Some camera views, like the one facing out from the building's front entrance, watched all foot traffic in and out of the facility. Other monitors flipped quickly through wide-angle camera shots, inside and out, rooftop to basement, front to back.

A large board littered with key hooks was on the wall behind the young guard's desk. Each location was clearly marked, and I spotted a silver key waiting below Base A. My mission was accomplished and my reward was to take up that can of sugar and caffeine.

After ten that night, I waited for Pat in my wheelchair. She finally bounced in and threw a towel and bottle of shampoo on my lap. Waving the key to the Beauty Shop, she pushed me out the door and up the hall. We passed the lone nurse on duty who ignored us to read reports.

Entering the elevator, we stayed quiet. While under surveillance, Pat and I knew not to act out of the ordinary or draw attention from the eyes now watching the monitors.

Leaving the elevator, we proceeded to the Beauty Shop. After Pat inserted the key, we rolled into the dark salon and were surprised by the ceiling lighting up. We looked around for cameras. One hung in the corner. It came on with the lights and was sweeping the room.

Pat explained the sudden lights, "Motion sensors come alive after visiting hours. They're in the doorways and all public areas. Management explains them as an insurance demand to avoid stumbling in the dark." She looked at me strangely and giggled, "Hey, don't I know someone who did that very same thing?"

"I know why the Chicago Mob threatened their enemies with a baseball bat to the knees."

Pat pushed me to a sink and had me bend my head back as she draped my shoulders with towels. The spray of warm water felt refreshing and I closed my eyes to enjoy the shampoo bubbling in my hair. Pat maneuvered her body in front of the camera which was my clue to speak freely. "Security has a key rack in the outer office. The old gym key is hanging at Base A."

"I brought putty with me to make an impression. Rainey has a guy who'll make copies."

"How're you going to get into Security?"

"You'll hear the fire alarm go off when the shift changes."

After the late night news, when I had settled in to watch Jimmy Kimmel start his monologue, the building alarms sounded with increasing urgency. Footsteps pounded up and down the corridors as hall speakers blurted out a recorded message from Director Wolfe:

THIS IS AN ALERT. ALL PATIENTS STAY IN YOUR ROOMS. STAFF WILL COME TO INFORM YOU WHAT TO DO. THIS IS NOT A DRILL.

Chapter Thirteen

The following day was scheduled for my return trip to the surgeon's office. I rode in the back of the medivan, enjoying the feel of sunshine and sounds of birdsong. Blooming flora generated feelings of hope for a brighter tomorrow full of healing physically and psychologically.

As I chitty chatted about the gorgeous Virginia countryside, Dr. Saville smiled. "I'm glad you're feeling better. Still, no standing or weight bearing on that knee. I'm going to let you take off your immobilizer so you can be wheeled into the shower. Would you like that?"

"Oh that would be so nice, but how can I do that in a wheelchair?"

"They have a special chair for their Shower room. They're quite safe."

"And will you please write down on that chart that I am no longer mentally unstable?"

"Oh, c'mon. What fun would that be?" He chuckled.

"They're treating me like I'm half crazy back there."

His handsome face fell into a big smile. "Don't you think we should keep it that way?"

I thought about the benefits of being left alone in my room. "You're right. Don't write a word about my sanity. Let 'em wonder. You do realize that I'm stable now, correct?"

Those blue eyes stared straight into mine and he dropped the humor. "Yes, I see it."

"And I can count on you to bail me out if they accuse me of unusual behavior?"

"If I can't come, I'll send in the cavalry." His smile reappeared and I felt safe again.

Returning to Barrington Hall, my daytime CNAs were excited to see that I could be pushed into the shower. It was Mary who put me on the evening shower list and laughed. "Now we can stop calling you, Stinky."

After working out in the darkened gym that evening, my sweaty body craved hot sudsy water. As I waited for Pat to come get me, a young girl wearing a trainee pin came in with a big smile. Jeanne, our evening nurse, followed and introduced Tara to me. "Would you mind if Tara took you to the shower."

Trying not to be conspicuous I asked, "What happened to Pat, my regular CNA?"

Jeanne was quick to explain. "We're short staffed on the Third Floor." I made a dumb face, looking for more information. "Our Third floor houses Alzheimer/Dementia patients and we are required to have a full crew up there."

My disappointment showed. "I imagine they must need a lot of care."

"We only allow more experienced staff to go upstairs. Pat's background is perfect."

"Hope she returns to the First Floor soon." I whined, while wondering what kind of references Pat was able to secure from Raines that gave her access to the mentally deranged?

Tara hummed as she pushed the shower chair into my room. Seeing it, I had to laugh. The big hole in the canvas seat made it look more like a toilet. I climbed aboard and Tara rolled me into the Shower Room. It had two exit doors across from each other to give access to either corridor. Along one wall was a row of curtained shower stalls. Tara guided me into the far end unit, explaining that it would be the warmest for my first shower. Once she had me inside with my chair wheels locked down, Tara left me alone behind the drawn curtain.

Taking off my hospital gown and then sitting in the chair nude made me feel vulnerable.

Tara's hand reached through the curtain and handed the shower head to me. "If you don't mind being by yourself, I'd like to run out and have a quick smoke?"

"Sure, go ahead. I'm fine." And I meant it.

My hands quickly adjusted the water temp and lifted the shower head. When the warm water pulsated over my body, I relaxed and let the wash rush over me. Feeling human again, I soaped up and sprayed away weeks of pain and anger. Once my skin felt clean, my eyelids felt heavy. When they fluttered shut, I fell back with the shower head still in my hand. Warm water sprayed down my legs and it was not long before I slipped into a dreamy state of mind. As the classic old tunes played overhead, my mind rolled back in time and tried to remember the lyrics.

Though deep in relaxation, I was distracted by a far away noise. My mind did not want to leave its sweet stupor to define where that sound had originated, but my rapid heartbeat demanded it. I heard it again and wondered if it was the squeak of a door opening?

When the room went dark, my eyes flew open. The only light came from the red radiance of the security lights. Holding my breath, I waited for someone, anyone, to announce his or her presence. Nothing! My ears began to pound as my blood pressure sped up. I tried to concentrate on the eerie silence punctuated by the soft spray of water until I heard something hit the floor.

I heard it again. Heavy footsteps wearing street shoes were coming my way, walking along the front of the stalls. The screech of metal scraping against metal made me jump. Someone was pushing the shower curtains across the rods. Someone was looking inside each stall. Someone was coming for me. Alone and frightened, I lost control of my bladder.

All I could do was wait ... wet and naked. Without thinking why, my hand reached down and picked up the shampoo bottle. The screech sounded from the stall beside me and I knew that I was next. Spinning off the cap, I held out the open end of the plastic bottle. When my curtain was swept back, a dark outline of a man stood in front of the red glow.

Against all orders, I stood up and squeezed the shampoo bottle with both hands. Aiming at the head, I heard the gurgle of thick shampoo shooting out and it sounded awful. The man's violent scream sounded worse.

Pain gripped my knee until I fell back in the chair. Looking up for my attacker, I could only see the red radiance lighting up the Shower Room. The shadow of the attacker had disappeared. Panting for breath and clutching my beating chest, I heard the closest door slam behind him and the faraway door open for Tara. I could hear her sweet voice still humming until her innocent voice called out, "Hey! Why's it so dark in here?"

The sounds of her slipping on the soapy floor and her body slamming down sickened me.

Chapter Fourteen

The following morning long before breakfast, Mary woke me. "You need to get dressed, pronto!" There was a worried look on her beautiful dark face. "I'm not fooling with you. Get your head off that pillow. This is serious. You and your girlfriend have been summoned to an early morning meeting in the Director's Conference Room."

I yawned and rolled over, "I need coffee."

"You two have brought a lot of attention to yourselves." Mary pulled out a clean sweat outfit from my wardrobe, threw it on the bed and moved the bed table closer. Pointing to the cup of coffee and small tub of warm water she said, "There's your coffee. Drink it down and clean up. Make sure you wash out your mouth. No dirty words today. They'll only get you in more trouble." Mary pulled the curtain around my bed and left the room.

My mind was swirling, wondering if they had found out about my connection with Pat. Running every encounter through my head, I decided that they must have picked up a connection when Pat took me downstairs. Still, her background info had been secured by Luc Raines. One thing the intel agencies did well was create a solid cover.

Fifteen minutes later, I was charged up with caffeine and waiting in my wheel chair when Mary returned. She still looked concerned and I almost got the feeling that she was distancing herself from me. "What do you know, Mary? What's going on?"

She picked up my purse and set it on my lap. "You may need this."

I clutched my hands on the rubber wheels, preventing the chair from being moved. Flipping both wheel locks, I stood my ground. "I'm not leaving until you talk to me!"

Mary came around and looked straight in my eyes. "It's all about those reports you two ladies keep signing. I don't know what your complaints are about, but you got the Big Guy involved now. And, that ain't good!"

I shook my head trying to understand. "So when you say my girlfriend ... that would be?"

"The patient who goes outside on the patio to smoke."

"Smoking?" I must have looked relieved. "Me? I'm not smoking!"

"Do you think I care whether you're smoking?"

"Yes. Darlene smokes, but I don't. Who said I was smoking?"

"Who cares?" She reached down and unlocked my wheels. "They're waiting downstairs."

As Mary pushed me along the hallway, past the empty Nurse's Station, I picked up a feeling of foreboding. Maybe, it was the odd silence as we rode down the elevator and exited below. Maybe, it was the odd silence as we traveled the basement corridor to the Conference Room. Maybe, it was the odd silence from Mary when I asked her to take me back to my room?"

Mary never stopped pushing me forward. "You don't have a choice. You're going!"

Heading into the large room, I saw that all the chairs had been pulled away from the long table centered under the ceiling lights. Shadowed faces sat back against the wall; some in medical garb, others in street clothes. Unable to see their full faces, I could only make out the features of my favorite nurse, Angela. She stared ahead without showing recognition.

Mary parked me next to Darlene who was already pulled up to the table. She, too, did not acknowledge me. Her eyes were on Kyle Marx, Wolfe's assistant, standing at the end of the table.

He looked upset, but even in anger Marx was a handsome black man with thick lashes over piercing eyes. Staring down at us, he did smile. "These reports have me worried, ladies"

I spoke up, "You should be worried. There's strange things going on around here?"

He stared down his nose at me. "I'm not sure that's true."

Darlene shouted, "Do you think we're telling lies?"

He put up his hands. "Now, I didn't say that. But, often our eyes play tricks on us."

I practically jumped out of my chair. "I know what I saw!"

Darlene backed me up. "We saw it together!"

When he leaned forward to check the reports in front of him, I caught a whiff of stale smoke. Had it been from a cigarette, I would have surmised that it encircled Darlene. No, this smoke was from a cigar ... an expensive cigar. Kyle Marx looked up and eyed me as if he had caught my thoughts. "You both have been here for awhile and ..."

Darlene interrupted, "Don't pull that crap on us. We know what we saw."

"And what did you see? Shadows? That's what it says here. You both saw shadows?"

Kyle twisted his face to show disgust. "And what happened last night in the Shower Room?" He squinted down at me, demanding my explanation.

"A man came in and turned off the lights. I heard big footsteps. He searched every stall until he found me, naked and all alone." Hearing my childlike narrative, I stopped.

Kyle smiled slyly. "Tara did not see a man enter the Shower Room and she was standing right outside in the hallway. Tara said there was a problem when the lights flickered. But for some unknown reason, Ms. Hennessey, you squirted shampoo all over the floor outside your shower stall." He waited for this crazy sounding chain of events take form for the listeners before he asked, "Is that correct?"

My answer was going to be tricky. I did not want to get Tara in trouble by saying that she had left me alone to go outside for a cigarette. "Please believe me. When the lights went out, there were footsteps coming at me and the shower curtains were being drawn back. I didn't have a weapon, so I used the shampoo to scare off the attacker when he got to my curtain."

Seeing both Kyle and Darlene's reactions, I realized how silly my explanation sounded.

"Ms. Hennessey, Tara ran to your aid when she heard your scream. She slipped in that shampoo. Her arm is broken. She won't be able to work for an extended amount of time."

"And I feel terrible about that, but I'm telling the truth. There was a man searching for me in the Shower Room." Looking around at the shadowy faces, I tried to get the heat off me. "Our real concern here is Genevieve. Darlene and I are asking that you pay special attention to her."

Before Marx could answer, his boss walked through the open door. Wilder Wolfe was even more handsome close up. His brown wavy hair held sun highlights that no stylist could create. The deep tan was earned outdoors ... sailing or tennis? I could only guess.

As Wolfe walked up to Marx, his deep blue eyes crossed over at us. "Good morning, ladies. I'm sorry to be late. Traffic is never an excuse until you have to cross the bridge."

Kyle looked eager to explain, "We were discussing these erroneous reports."

Darlene and I were still staring at Director Wolfe, who looked around and used his big smile to warm up the room.

Kyle stepped back when it looked like Wolfe would take over. "Ladies," he smiled down at the two of us, "tell me what happened."

Darlene could hardly get her thoughts out, but finally relayed how we saw someone pull Genevieve away from the window. I jumped in to tell how a man wanted to check my diaper.

Kyle smirked, the night shift makes rounds to change diapers, Ms. Hennessey."

"I don't wear diapers and staff reported that there were no males on duty that night!"

Wolfe glanced at the onlookers and somehow picked up their silent inference. He turned back to the two of us. "Ladies, I believe you. Kyle will open an investigation."

All eyes went to Marx's surprised face. "Of course, Wilder. That's a good idea."

Darlene and I smiled our gratitude at the Director, but still there was that sweet woman who could not speak for herself. I asked, "What are you going to do about Genevieve?"

Kyle waved off our concern. "We're giving her a roommate who'll keep an eye on her."

I felt some relief, but Darlene looked perturbed. "Have you decided who it'll be?"

Kyle smiled wide, taking full credit. "Sister Elizabeth."

Chapter Fifteen

After the meeting, Darlene and I wheeled out to the patio where we locked our wheels. Her hands were visibly shaking; no doubt she was in need of nicotine. Using her gold lighter, Darlene lit the tip of her cigarette and took a deep drag. The soothing smoke curled in and out of her mouth with her next breaths. Not getting it fast enough, she sniffed her exhaled smoke back up her nostrils. I remembered that sacred ritual as if my last cigarette was put out yesterday.

Like all smokers, Darlene did her best thinking with a cigarette between her fingers while smoke filled her lungs. Watching her, I could almost feel her rising blood pressure and racing heartbeat until the nicotine hits the brain and gives every smoker a rush. And that rush lets the mind of the smoker open up and to the secrets of the world. Watching all of this transpire for Darlene, I realized once again how much I missed smoking.

Waiting for her to relax, I looked around at the empty tables and chairs. Since it was so early in the day, we were alone. Because the patio was a public area on the facility's grounds, I assumed there was surveillance. Although I could not remember seeing film from the patio flip on the security monitors, I was certain that devices were planted all around us. Unable to get up and search the bushes and lighting fixtures, I began with mundane conversation until I noticed Darlene's newly polished nails. "Hey, where'd you get your nails done?"

She looked anxious and clearly did not want to engage in small talk. "Volunteers come in weekly and do them for nothing." Taking another drag off her smoke she sighed. "I don't like what just went on in there. I suppose we're being watched even now." Her head nodded to the building behind us. "Those two men are not what they pretend to be. I can't put my finger on it, but something's not right here." Before I could agree, she rushed ahead. "I can't stomach that Kyle Marx." She stuck out her tongue demonstrating the bitter taste of his name coming out of her mouth, but then she gave me a funny look. "And, what the hell happened last night in the Shower Room?"

I told her every detail and ended by asserting, "Hard to believe, I know, but it's the truth."

"I believe you, but the Assistant Director wanted to make you out as a liar."

"And why would he want to do that?"

"To keep his job, probably. Anything major goes wrong here and Wolfe'll eat him alive."

I looked shocked and Darlene realized what she had just said. The ghastly visual pushed both of us into laughter. We laughed so hard that we fell into choking fits. Trying to catch our breath, we looked away from each other to gain control of ourselves.

Glancing back at the patio door leading into the cafeteria, I spotted Kyle Marx inside. He stood alone in the shadows, but I could make out his eyes looking straight at us. Turning back, I whispered to Darlene. "Don't look now, but Kyle is standing inside the glass door staring at us."

We pretended to look around at the lush greenery growing along the edge of the cliff and listen to the rushing sounds of the river below until Kyle's face disappeared.

Darlene kept smoking, one cigarette after another. Speaking out of the corner of her mouth she said, "Meg, I have a confession." I kept still and waited. "My reports were not quite accurate." I did not react. "Remember, I told you about that masked man creeping around my room one night?" I nodded. "Never did report that incident. Didn't want 'em to think I was nuts."

I had to giggle at her innocence. "They already think we're nuts!"

Smoke blew out with her burst of laughter. "When I think about what's happening here? Even I wonder if we're not nutty. You gotta admit that shower-room-story of yours is a doozey?"

I tried to explain between gagging on my own laughter, "It does sound strange and no one wants to believe me, but I was terrorized last night."

"I believe you! I believe you!" Her eyes lit up with her devious smile. "Bet Tara and her broken arm believe you, too." She winked and again her edgy humor put us into silly laughter.

Feeling guilty, I stopped. "Oh, that poor kid's arm. I do feel awful about her fall."

Darlene waved off my concern. "You want to know what I feel awful about?" My face went blank. "The way those men who run this joint want to sweep our complaints under the rug."

Chapter Sixteen

The next day was all downhill for me. I did not want to wake up or eat my breakfast. My sense of humor was nowhere to be found. During physical therapy, I never smiled when Darlene made faces at Cheryl's back. Nor when Cheryl caught her and made faces back at Darlene.

When it became time to work out with Beck, he eyed me strangely and I snapped at him. "Stop looking at me. I'm sick of being stared at and I'm sick of being here for your gratification!"

He tried to make a joke. "You American girls, always turning things around."

"What do you mean by that?"

His put his hands on his hips. "You think I'm here for my gratification. The reason I'm here, young lady, is to get you walking again." He winked, trying to cover his caustic manner.

Beck was right of course. Deep down I knew that I was suffering with a case of self pity.   For the first time since Pat had brought in a new cell phone, I had used it to call my old number late last night. My lost phone was important to me. It held the last voice messages left by my husband. Many times when I desperately needed to hear the sound of his voice, I dialed him up and last night was one of them. When the lost cell allowed me to leave a message, I assumed that the battery was still charged and it was not in anyone's possession. The message that I had left spelled out the generous reward to anyone who would call me back from that phone.

After I had called my old cell, I could not stop my fingers from dialing my dead husband's personal phone ... the cell number that I kept paying for in order to insure his voice stayed alive long after his ashes went into the ground. My heartbeat stopped to listen to his quip: *Ya better leave your name and number or I'll have you tracked down.*

Hearing his genuine laughter and promise to call back had once again been bittersweet. And like always, I left yet another message for him to *please come back and track ME down.* Only this time I added my new cell number. It did not matter that his phone was laying untouched in his top dresser drawer, and that no one would ever listen to my messages.

And while this insane activity served to remind me of what I used to have, it also reminded me of what I had lost. Like an addict, I accepted the manic high and low of this activity. And as always, an odd voice in the back of my head accepted that most living spouses of the deceased practiced this same ritual now that we were in the new age of technical miracles.

I looked up to see Beck waiting for me to get up on the table. Climbing out of my chair, I kept my eyes away from him. As he led me through our foot pushes and leg raises, I kept my eyes down. My pouty profile was all he was going to get and I could not wait for my time with the man to end so I could go back to my room and sulk.

Lunch and dinner trays came and went looking the same both ways. My appetite for food or life had disappeared. Why I wanted to return to the gym that evening was beyond my comprehension. No doubt laying in bed for so many days with nothing to do, but watch brain-dead television drove me to it. So, I transported my stiff body into the chair and had a long cry.

It was quiet in Barrington Hall after visiting hours as I wheeled along the corridors. Since the ceiling lights were turned down, there was no glare in my eyes and I could almost imagine that I was not in a rehabilitation facility. Going into the dark gym felt especially cathartic that evening. Maybe it was being alone and in command of my actions that made me feel free.

I pulled up to the training table and wiggled my body onto it without standing on my legs. The firm leather felt cool as I flattened my shoulders back to rest and collect my energy. Laying with my hands above my head and eyes half-closed, it felt even better. Soothing music began to play over the ceiling speakers. There was no pattern to our in-house concerts nor was there a specific music style played. Tonight, a series of Henry Mancini's movie themes were the venue. I remembered them all from seeing the magnificent films with my parents. No doubt the memorable tunes from decades past were used to lull the aging residents into falling deep asleep.

Listening to the old favorites and guessing the film titles, I felt relaxed until an alarm went off in my head. I turned to look into the Daily Living Quarters located beyond the gym and saw a shadowy movement. At first, I thought my eyes were mistaken. Then I wondered if someone might be in the space created as a household setting. Since I could only see through the arched doorway into the dining room, I dismissed the apparition as an illusion.

Still, I kept my ears open for strange noise above the soft music. Closing my eyes again, I plotted my PT routine and how many repetitions I felt up to performing. Sleep must have overtaken me because when I awoke, my mental clock had ticked off several lost minutes. The music was no longer playing and I had an empty feeling of being alone.

Stretching, I began to slide my backside across the table toward my chair. It did not take long for me to see that my mode of transportation was no longer there. Scanning the darkened gym to see if it might have rolled, it became clear to me that my chair was nowhere in sight.

While wondering who would have left me stranded, I heard sirens and the sounds of large vehicles making their way up the long drive from Georgetown Pike. Since we were accustomed to ambulances coming and going at odd times, I did not pay too much attention. When loud yelling and running erupted in the hall, I became anxious to know what was happening.

I had my cell and tried to call Pat, but her end kept going to voice mail. Just before I was ready to drop to the floor on my good leg and crawl across the floor, her shadow came running into the gym. Seeing her pony tail swaying I called out, "What's going on?"

She ran up and was out of breath, "Genevieve's been murdered in her bed!"

"Oh no, where was Sister Elizabeth?"

"She went to pray in the library with some of her nuns."

My heart began to race and I felt rage. "How was Genevieve killed?"

"Her throat was slashed, ear to ear. It's a mess and there'll be one hell of an investigation." She looked around. "I've got to get you back to your room. Where's your chair?"

"You tell me? I must've dozed off. When I awoke, it was gone."

Pat looked frightened. "I'll go get you a chair from the old gym. Stay here."

I had to smile at her order. "You're kidding, right?"

Before she could enjoy her pun, Kyle stuck his head in and yelled. "Police are here. They ordered us to stay right where we are until they can question everyone." He turned away, dashing down the hall. We could hear him shouting out the same instructions along the way.

Pat climbed up on the training table next to me. "This'll cause a shit storm!"

"Are your credentials and resume going to hold up to police scrutiny?"

"Yes. If not, Rainey will give me back-up."

"He won't like having to brief the local authorities as to why you're here."

She nodded and looked concerned. "Let's go over the stuff that can put us in jeopardy."

"Hey, I'm here legit. If your credentials can pass muster, we're clean."

"There's that bag in your wardrobe. All of it can be innocently explained away."

"True and any other stuff that might be in the duffel could be there from previous trips?"

"Right!" Her face brightened. "And tell the truth about what you've seen and heard around here. Can't lie. Wolfe's got your signed reports. What about the cell I gave you?"

I showed her that it was still in my hand. "It'll show I just tried to call you?"

"That's okay. Most CNAs give their cell numbers to their patients. We hate that damn buzzing at the Nurse's Station." She made an ugly face. "And tell how you woke up to find your chair missing. That puts you here." She looked at me funny, "How do you think that happened?"

"When I first arrived, I thought I spotted movement in the Daily Living Quarters."

Pat slid off the table and went through the arched doorway. Flipping on the lamps, she walked around. At the same time, a uniformed officer entered the gym. The man spotted Pat over there and held up a clipboard. "Hey, come back. I need your statement."

Pat returned wearing her sweetest smile ... the one with all her dimples, the one that had already charmed the young officer.

After we had answered all his questions, the three of us discussed Genevieve's cruel attack and I could only hope that the poor lady was deep asleep when death overtook her.

Chapter Seventeen

It was long after midnight when the police and fire department began the sweep of the first floor. We were informed that our rooms and all our belongings were being searched. Both Pat and I gave our statements to several more officers as to where we were during the evening.

While waiting in the gym for the authorities to release us, Pat asked how I was surviving.

"I'm at the backend of my time here and can't wait to begin walking again."

"I've been worried about you, but tried to leave you alone to recuperate." She put her arm around my shoulders. "It won't be long and we'll be driving around Georgetown again."

We broke into giggles. "Don't tell me we'll be doing more trash trips?"

"It's the staple of our business." She smiled. "I can't do them without you."

"Let's finish up the Luc Raines job here and look for cleaner contracts."

"There's always spying on the unfaithful?"

I felt disgust crawl across my face. "You're kidding, right?"

"Of course, we made that pact when we opened up. Don't worry, I'm working on getting new work. Right now, all I want you to do is heal so you can walk out of here."

We caught up on small talk until the original officer returned. He gave Pat the all clear and she left to get another wheelchair. As I sat alone, running the evening events through my head, my mind stopped at the exact moment when I sensed a presence near me. My stomach acid erupted and tasted bitter when I wondered. "Could I have been able to scare off the attacker?"

Pat pushed me into my room and I could see the excitement in her eyes as she said, "When I went to the Security Office to let me in the old gym, the coppers were watching tonight's surveillance tapes. Someone wearing scrubs, surgical net and sunglasses rode out the front door and past the cameras in your wheelchair. Better yet, while the guard was digging around for a good wheelchair in Base A, I tried my new copy of the key and it works."

She pulled out the silver chain hanging around her neck. "No doubt I'll have to go through a pat-down before I walk out here." For some reason that made me laugh. "You're laughing at Pat getting a pat-down, right?" I nodded and her eyes rolled. "Please make the person tall, handsome and male."

I added, "And a rich widower over forty might be nice too."

Handing me the necklace she said, "Hide this somewhere."

Sleeping alone in my room that night was not easy. All bedroom doors were ordered to stay open and the ceiling lights in the corridors were turned up. Marching feet never stopped rushing up and down the halls answering patient calls. Personnel came into my room often, always waving flashlights. As the sun finally rose, I looked forward to morning coffee.

When Lyrie arrived, I smiled. "Good to see you. What a night!"

She bent over the bed and hugged me. "I heard. And you were caught in the gym?"

"Without my chair! Did they tell you that?" I sounded like a whiny kid.

"Yes. Did you know they found your chair out in the field. The murderer used it to get past the Nurse's Station." She lowered her voice, "When those nurses hear rubber wheels, they don't even turn around or look up."

"Tell me they got a good surveillance picture of the guy?"

"They got a grainy photo. The police were waiting for us when we took over the shift and showed it to us, but it's not clear. The film's black and white. They reuse the tapes to save money and it looks blurry. None of us recognized the person."

"But it is a man, a white man?"

"With dark glasses and hair net? It's hard to say. Couldn't swear to the skin color either."

"Lyrie, did anything about the murderer seem familiar to you?"

"Yes, but don't ask me what it is because so many people wander around this place."

"How about the clothing; anything special?"

"Blue scrubs worn over a lean body is all I could make out."

I felt frustration rise. "Darlene and I warned everyone that Genevieve was in danger."

"Try not to think about it. Let the authorities find the killer and let me get your coffee."

After breakfast, a pair of nurses that I had never seen before came to question me. Without introducing themselves, they explained how they were visiting all the patients after last night's *disturbance*. Wearing phony smiles, they strongly suggested the benefit of group counseling now being offered every evening in the cafeteria.

The shorter one commented on my dark circles, suggesting sleeping pills to get a good night's rest. She coyly brought up the possibility that I might be contemplating a move to another facility? The taller one piped up, "And who would blame you?"

Nodding, I smiled. "All good things to think about." They promptly got up and left.

When it came time for me to go for PT, my stomach churned. I knew how disgusted I felt about Genevieve's murder and could only wonder how Darlene was reacting to it.

Surprisingly, when I wheeled into the gym Darlene was there and waved. Parking beside her, I sensed her anxiety and let her open the conversation. Blowing out an imaginary puff of cigarette smoke she shook her head. "We told 'em, didn't we?"

"Oh yes, we tried. Any ideas on who did it?"

"I know exactly who did it."

Turning to look into her eyes I asked, "What do you mean?"

"My boyfriend, Harold, loved switchblades. Silent and deadly and that's his direct quote."

My heart climbed into my mouth. "You don't think he's been the attacker here?"

"I've no doubt that Genevieve was easy prey for that sicko who kept trying to get into all of our diapers." Her eyes looked sad. "But, I also know that Harold wanted to take me out."

"I'm confused. Why would Harold want to kill Genevieve?"

"When I first came here, I landed in Genevieve's bed. They moved me out of that room to make space for two male patients. After they left, Genevieve was put in my old bed."

"Oh no! So, you feel it was Harold who killed Genevieve thinking it was you?"

Darlene was already nodding with tears glistening in her eyes. I saw her lips mouth a foul slur containing two words to describe her boyfriend. The first was *mother*.

"There's security pictures of the murderer leaving through the front door."

"I haven't seen them yet. Have you?" Darlene asked.

"No, but my CNA described the bastard. Lean body under scrubs, surgical net and shades. She said the security photos were so bad, she couldn't tell male or female, white or black. Does any of that sound like Harold?"

"Harold's a chameleon and yes he's Jack-Sprat thin, metabolism of a bird. Spent his younger years robbing banks. Walked right up to tellers and never got fingered by surveillance."

"Why would he want to kill you, Darlene?"

"My boys told me the piece-of-crap cashed me out and left the apartment."

"You've got to get a look at those security photos."

"Wolfe and Marx'll never let the patients see them. They're already bracing for law suits."

"Contact the cops. They'd show them to you if they think you can help solve this crime."

"Huh, the cops? Those county boys won't get him nor the molester working inside here."

"What if it is Harold and he comes back to finish the job?" I had to ask.

Her eyes went from sad to mad. The evil snarl working its way around her lips frightened me. "Don't worry, I'll be waiting."

Chapter Eighteen

A dark cloud loomed over Barrington Hall after Genevieve was found murdered. Everyone felt that in some small way that we had let the poor woman down. No longer were the staff and patients joking around with each other. Friendly chatter in the corridors and laughter in the gym disappeared. Suspicion and fear crept over us all. The facility lost its warmth and felt cold as a morgue. I guess we could have been considered its walking dead.

Visiting Dr. Saville had always been my outlet to the real world, but on this day I needed a dose of his warm charm. The man was fun and easy to tease because he liked to tease back. I brightened when he walked in and said, "So kiddo, you still having fun over at Barrington?"

"More fun than I can stand." He did not smile. "You heard about the murder mystery?"

"Who didn't?" His blue eyes opened wide. "Have they found the guy yet?"

"No, and doubtful they will ever get to the bottom of what happened."

"They must have some ideas. What about the rumors?"

"Everyone's got an opinion. Some say a fox got into the hen house. Others think it was a case of mistaken identity."

He gave me a sincere smile. "I don't like it. Seems depressing. There's other facilities we can transfer you to that are just as good. How about we move you out of there?"

I pointed to my newly taken x-rays. "How many weeks do I have left before I can walk?"

He turned around to review the wispy image of my knee. "Looks great. I'm going to let you take off the immobilizer and start on a walker." He saw my exuberance and put up his hand. "Take it slow. Don't hurt yourself. Let your therapists guide you. You'll need a week or two to learn how to get around, but I'll release you to go home if you can walk steadily on a walker. Then, we'll get Home Health to work with you. Does that sound like a plan?"

I wanted to kiss him and not just for giving me an escape route. The man was a genuinely a good soul and a friend that I had come to admire and trust. "That sounds wonderful!"

He pulled out his script pad and began squiggling. "You're going to need pain medication when you put weight on that leg. Even more when they begin to work on that scar tissue. Don't be a heroine. Take the meds." He winked. "Come see me in two weeks." When I began to push the wheelchair towards the door he said, "And next time, I want to see you walk in the door."

Traveling back in the medivan felt exhilarating The late summer breeze smelled floral fresh and felt soft against my skin. With approval to begin walking in my hand, I could endure another short descent into hell. In no time, I vowed to be flying around on the walker.

When I wheeled into the gym and gave Beck my new orthopedic orders, he smiled. "We can get you mobile with the walker in a week."

I hopped on the training table and smiled, "Take off this leg brace and let's get started."

Since it was after two in the afternoon and most patients had drifted back to their rooms, Beck and I had the place to ourselves. He pulled back the Velcro straps and I winced feeling the air touching my newly exposed skin. I could see the atrophy after weeks of being bandaged. Beck worked with me for two hours, stretching and pulling both legs. Finally, he brought over a folded walker and I watched how he locked it into position.

Satisfied, he smiled and pointed to it. "Your chariot awaits."

Stepping onto the floor with both feet felt awkward and I kept my weight on the good leg. Beck let me stand by the table to regain my balance before he beckoned me to step forward. Smiling like a proud father he said, "Lead with your good leg and slide your other foot up to it."

Slowly, I continued forward. Holding on to the bars, my feet followed his command.

Walking backwards, he led me in circles around the empty gym. My steps sped up as we made the fifth go-around. He stopped me at the door. "You're bending forward and putting your weight on the bar of the walker. Straighten your back. Keep a light touch and push the walker."

We made another circle and it hit me that after all this time I was truly walking on my own. As I kept my fingers pushing the walker, I could no longer hold back my joy, "Yippee!"

Beck patted me on the shoulder. "You can walk back to your room now. No more chair."

Moving slowly down the hall, I made it to my door feeling as if I had won a marathon.

Conquering the walker served to open many opportunities for me over the next few days, including the ability to travel into my own bathroom. Not only could I dispense with the commode, but the sink offered availability to take spit baths. Since I had vowed never to go back in the Shower Room, this excited me. My daily routine kept changing for the better.

My stiff knee swelled and felt on fire after working out with Beck every day. The pain meds were timed to reach me as soon as we finished and when it was time to sleep. When the nurses ran to me holding out the pills, I could not get them down fast enough. Still, pushing the walker instead of rubber wheels felt heavenly.

Because Beck kept me coming to the gym after two in the afternoon, I no longer had morning sessions. He said that my upper-body exercises had ended. Not working with Cheryl meant not seeing Darlene. And while I could have found Darlene in her room or the cafeteria or the patio, I never went looking for her. My focus was on my own improvement and going home.

Mixing with the others still did not appeal to me even though I could easily access the cafeteria and public areas. Seeing so many drooping heads and lackluster eyes made me wonder if many of the patients were being fed *downers* to keep them docile? This frightening thought kept me ever vigilant over my own meds. I knew the size and color of every pill prescribed.

Readying to rejoin the outside world, I spent time now talking on the phone with loved ones who lived in the Midwest. I no longer minded questions and readily explained the slippery fall that caused my injury. I could laugh at their jibes because now I had a happy ending to share.

Pat bounced in late one evening holding a towel and shampoo. "Ready to go downstairs and get your hair washed?"

Although I had already donned my hospital gown for the night, I quickly got out of bed and grabbed my robe. Before we left, I pulled out my purse from the wardrobe. Tucked inside the lining were two keys. One was for my house in case my key ring ever got misplaced. The second was the Base A key that Pat had copied. I handed the necklace to her and she smiled.

Walking along the hallway, my hands kept a light touch on the walker rolling in front of me. Waving to the duty nurse, we entered the elevator and made small talk as we rode down.

When the doors opened to the basement, the corridor was dark. I followed Pat to the Beauty Shop where she used the key she got from the Nurse's Station to unlock the door. Walking inside set off the motion sensors, turning on the ceiling lights and starting up the corner camera to continuously sweep the room.

Although I was sure that Pat had ulterior motives, I needed to get my hair washed and sat in the chair. Leaning my head back in the sink, I watched her maneuver so that her back faced the camera. She bent over and whispered, "We're going into the old gym tonight."

My shoulders slumped, but there was no arguing. "Do you know what we're looking for?"

"We need to nosey around. Beck's not told us a thing lately and Rainey wants answers."

"I don't think Beck knows any more. This place's tighter than a drum since the murder."

"Yeah. The cops have nowhere to go with that case either. It may never get solved."

"Genevieve's murderer might not be found! Where'd you get your information?"

"Neal's friends on the force gave it to me straight." Her eyes looked as sad as I felt.

I toyed with the idea of giving up Darlene's theory regarding the homicide to Pat, but thought better of it. That intel could be delivered to the police after I was safely back at home. Right then, Pat and I had to concentrate on securing information for Luc Raines to fulfill our contract. Seeing Pat deep in thought as she lathered up my hair, allowed me to close my eyes.

Several minutes later, I felt the warm water rinse turn cold. The joy of this soothing ritual was over. I opened my eyes and asked, "Okay partner. What's your plan?"

"First, I'm going to rip off one of your wheels." Pat laughed at my quizzical look. "There's only one guard on duty. Unless there's an emergency, he has to stay in the office to man the phones and watch the monitors. I'll ask him for the key. If he lets us go to the old gym alone? Great. If he doesn't we'll use plan B."

As Pat faked dropping the towel and bending down to pick it up, she reached out to my walker and unscrewed a back wheel. Standing up, she threw the towel on my head and her strong hands dried my hair with vigor. We joked about her vicious scalp rubbing until she continued the charade by pointing to the missing wheel.

I looked down and pretended to be surprised, "What're we going to do?"

"Stay here, there's extra pieces in the old gym. I'll go ask Security for the key."

Pat flew out the door, forgetting the sensor would automatically turn off the ceiling lights. With wet hair dripping in my eyes, I felt panic rising and my hands shaking. The toll that the long recuperation had taken on my nerves proved how much I needed to get away from Barrington Hall.

The door opened and the lights came on again. Pat laughed, teasing me. "You look silly sitting alone in the dark. Why didn't you get up and wave your hand or just flip on the lights?"

Turning my head away from the camera I told her why. "You dismantled my walker!"

With her divine finesse, Pat turned from prankster to penitent. "Forgive me?"

"Only if you help me out of this beauty-parlor chair."

I was able to push the limping contraption that used to be my walker all the way to the door of Base A, where Pat inserted the key given her by the guard. When the door to the old gym opened, Pat entered without sensors lighting up. This area still needed to have the lights switched on the old fashioned way. Pat hit the switch and I followed her inside as we both looked around.

Chapter Nineteen

Stepping gingerly, Pat and I made our way around the clutter awaiting us inside. Although it appeared that this unused area was even larger than the working gym upstairs, it was hard to tell as there were so many pieces of outdated gymnastic contraptions piled on top of each other.

We both eyeballed the corners and ceilings, looking for cameras. She was the first to say that the room might have been closed off before the security system had been installed.

I wondered aloud, "How old is this place?"

Pat answered without turning around. "They're celebrating twenty-years next week."

"Oh yeah, how can they celebrate at a rehab facility?"

"It's a surprise, but there's plans underway for a big party next Saturday."

"I'm only interested if they're serving alcohol." We chided back and forth, but kept making our way along an uncluttered trail that was so narrow that we were forced to walk single file. I pushed my sluggish walker without a back wheel and limping on my own behind Pat.

Every few steps, she turned to survey my progress. "You okay back there, Gimpy?"

"Gimpy?" I had to laugh along with her. "You'd find humor at a martyr's funeral."

"It's part of our Irish heritage. I'd like to think that our poor Celtic ancestors laughed through the famine." Something caught her eye and she pointed to the side wall on the right.

Seeing boxes piled up to the ceiling, I sighed. "Do we have to check every one?"

"I'll do it. You go look for a workbench or equipment drawers. We need to find a wheel for your walker." Pushing her way to the pile-up, I heard her throwing boxes at break-neck speed. Without stopping, she hollered back to me. "What was that crazy name again?"

I could still recall that razor sharp word that Beck had whispered to me. "Mortez!"

"I don't like the sound of it. Gives me chills. Let's hope the box is still here."

"Still here?" I had to laugh. "Every box ever delivered is still here." I kept limping along, looking for a work bench. Up ahead was a clearing where I found several gunmetal cabinets pushed up against the back wall. I began to scrounge through the unlocked drawers, looking for a matching wheel, when an obvious question hit me. "Hey Pat, what happened to the wheel you removed from my walker?"

"The guard had it in his hand when the phone rang. While he was distracted, I grabbed the key off the hook." Her hearty laugh followed. "I got out of there in a hurry. Sorry."

Opening the next drawer, I saw a variety of wheels. "This is your lucky day. I got one!"

Turning around, Pat was standing behind me and holding up a box. "So did I!"

We looked closer at the Connecticut Avenue return address and suite number. "Rainey will be excited." Although she ripped out the piece that contained it, we instinctively read it again and memorized the address. "I'll deliver this to Luc personally."

I sighed, "And that's our last deliverable on his contract. We've earned our money, right?"

"Yep. Perfect timing too cause you'll be blowing this place soon."

"So are you?" I did not like the way she turned away. "Why would you stay here, Pat?"

"Rainey said he'd add another task to our contract once we found this address."

Before I could question her further, she tucked the piece of cardboard inside her bra and stepped to the side of the cabinet. Scrutinizing the wall behind it, she dropped down on her knees and peered below. Jumping up, she grabbed the cabinet and pulled it away from the wall.

"What're you doing?" I was shocked at her strength.

"I see something back there." She pushed the cabinet again and exposed a door painted over to match the wall. "Look there's no knob, and the hinges must be on the other side."

"Let's leave it alone."

Too late, Pat scrambled through the drawers until she pulled out a heavy duty screw driver. Using it as a wedge, she popped the door away from the wall. When she pulled the door open, all we could see was darkness.

Pat whistled."What the hell is this?" Her eyes lit up and she took a tentative step inside. She pulled out her penlight, but it offered little illumination inside the darkness. "Wait here!"

Before I could stop her, Pat had already taken several steps and I lost sight of her. Frightened for her safety I screamed into the tunnel, "Are you okay?"

"I'm fine." She whispered back. "Stay there."

As I waited in the eerie silence, the sound of the hallway door creaking open took me by surprise. I could only assume that it was the guard coming in to check on us or to return the wheel Pat had left behind? Wanting to be prepared, my mind got busy. I tried to create a reason why I was there alone and why Pat was off exploring.

Without warning, the lights went out and I was left alone in the dark. Seconds seemed like minutes. Standing there, unable to make a sound, was hellish. Finally, I heard the door slam shut. But, was I alone again?

The silence made my ears ring. Feeling deaf and blind made my imagination want to play tricks. Drawn to the dark abyss, I called out to Pat in a whisper, but there was no response. A few steps more and I was inside. Taking tiny steps with my hands out to feel my way, I began my trek. When my fingertips were able to reach the interior walls, I hoped my claustrophobia would not force me to turn around. Still, I kept going and calling out. "Can you hear me, Pat?"

Without knowing whether the person who turned off the lights ever left the old gym, I could not help but sense danger. Real or not, my heart pounded as I hobbled along. Growing fear energized me and I picked up speed, skipping with one leg while dragging the other. When I slammed into a brick wall, I tasted blood. My nose must have gotten the worst of the bang.

Using my hands to feel my way, I found that the tunnel turned on a right angle. Now as I traveled this new passageway, my eyes squinted into even more darkness and my feet perceived a slight incline. Calculating how the tips of my fingers barely touched the walls, and how the human arm span matches height, I figured that the tunnel's width was five and a half feet.

I tried to reach up, but my hands only felt air above me. I wondered why this tunnel was created? Tired and scared, I stopped to catch my breath and call out again. "Pat! Where are you?"

Instead of her voice coming back to me, there was a distant sound of running. The footfalls were getting louder, gaining on me. I turned around to travel back to the old gym, but had to move cautiously as I worried about not hitting a wall again when the path turned left.

The runner's steps were gaining on me and I kept wondering who it could be other than Pat. I wanted to stop and call out again, but a new sound was added to the cacophony already playing in my head ... animal grunting. Fear of the unknown could not compete against my knee pain, now forcing me to slow down. And when I caught my breath, I figured out that the grunting was coming from inside my own body.

As I hippity-hopped along, I could feel the towel slipping from around my head. When it slid down my back, I let it fall behind in order to keep going. Running now with my hands out in front, I plowed into the wall that I had wanted to dodge. At the same time, I heard a thud behind me. I stopped to listen before I whispered again, "Pat?"

"Yes!" She yelled back adding her favorite cuss words. "Is this your towel I tripped on?"

Exiting the tunnel, Pat closed the door behind us and ran up front to turn on the lights. I rewrapped the towel around my head and when Pat returned, she pushed back the cabinet. We talked about the tunnel as she bent down and replaced the rear wheel on the walker.

She was excited to tell me, "That tunnel runs to the parking lot at the far end of the property. All I can figure is that it must've been created for easy access during construction."

"Deliveries by hand trucks could still roll through it." I added.

"The deliveries I see come through the double-door entry off the cafeteria." Pat shook her head. "I doubt that it's used for outside deliveries now. The steel door to the lot has a heavy sliding bolt lock built on the inside."

"I ran into the wall twice at the turn."

Pat stood up and eyed the perfectly aligned wheel on the walker. A bright smile smoothed over her face looking at her accomplishment. "There's a crossroad further down that I suspect lead one way to the main kitchen and the other to the laundry area. I have a hunch this tunnel is used to push laundry carts and the trash bins from the kitchen."

"That would make sense. What about the soiled linen rooms on each floor?" I asked.

"Yep, they all have giant laundry shoots leading down to the basement."

"And the main kitchen can use the tunnel to haul bulk food in and trash out." I added   We   ruminated   on   our discoveries until I asked, "Why were you running back?"

"Towards the end of the tunnel it widens. I sensed something down there, hiding in the dark. Whatever it was felt so sinister that if you hadn't been waiting? I wouldn't have turned around and come back in that tunnel."

"Was the door bolted when you opened it?"

Pat tapped her forehead. "Good thinking! No, I literally ran into it and it was not locked. But, I sure as hell threw that bolt across the door before I took off running back to you."

"Do you think someone was out in the lot ready to sneak back in and you surprised him?"

"Anything is possible?" She looked closer. "You got a bloody nose?"

"My first time walking in the dark."

"Wish you hadn't followed me." Her tone was soft.

"As soon as you left, the door to the hall opened. Someone stepped in and turned off the lights. When I heard the door close again, I guessed at first that it was the guard checking on us. But then, I would have sworn to our dead husbands that I heard someone coming after me in the dark gym. And that's when my imagination may have taken over and I ran into the tunnel."

Pat pushed the four-wheeled walker over to me. Reaching inside the v-neck of her uniform, she pulled out the piece of ripped cardboard hidden inside her bra. "Thought for sure this fell out with all that running."

Laughing I said, "Don't worry, we'll never forget that address."

Chapter Twenty

Although everyone inside the facility buzzed about the upcoming Saturday Celebration for Barrington Hall's twentieth birthday, the mood was subdued. The yellow tape sealing Genevieve's door and the continued police presence put everyone on edge. Officers in or out of uniform kept returning to dig for information regarding the murder.

On Friday morning, two such types came into my room and found me sitting in the only comfy chair in the room, sipping the last of my morning coffee.

"Ms. Hennessey? May we speak with you?"

When I looked up, both females had their county badges out for my perusal. They gave me a few seconds to take a long look at their credentials and their faces. I sized them up as two hardboiled officers who had no doubt put their time in at patrolling the county jail.

The beanpole with red hair looked strange next to the squat brunette. Forgettable in a crowd, they were perfect for detective work. Wearing mannish haircuts and no makeup, no one would remember their features. I stopped my mental criticism of the women thinking how my own face needed a facial and my pinned-up hair needed a dye job.

When they stepped closer, the redhead smiled. "Listen Meg, may I call you Meg?"

"No!"

"Thank you, Meg." She ignored my answer. "We know you're a registered PI. So, let's cut through the crap. If you're working on case in here, you better let us in on it."

The little rodent snickered, showing her pointy teeth. "You know we can pull your license for refusing to cooperate." Her snarl showed off the tiny hairs lining her upper lip and for the first time in my life ... I wished that I owned a cat.

"Check my medical records," I threw back at them. "You'll see I arrived as a cripple." I had to laugh. "You think I'd break my knee just to come here for a case." I shook my head.

Before I could say more, the little rat softened her approach. "We would naturally appreciate anything your trained eye might have picked up. After all, a defenseless woman...."

The redhead cut in, "What *can* you tell us about the old-lady killing?"

"Did you read my report in Wolfe's office?" They looked dumbfounded. "I filled out an Incident Report describing what I saw in Genevieve's window days before she was killed." Still, they stood shaking their heads. "Wolfe didn't discuss any of this with the police?"

Red sighed, as if she was forced to admit. "The Administration has been uncooperative."

"Tell us what was in your report?" The furry partner now tried to act as if we were pals.

"I gave all this information to your officer on the night of the murder." Outrage surpassed my aggravation. "Geez, I spent an hour with that guy. Don't tell me that report got lost too?"

The redhead moved closer. "We'd like to hear it again."

I repeated the facts without mentioning Darlene's name nor her take on Harold. "There's not a lot to tell. Genevieve was never able to speak, but always looked scared and screamed out as if begging for help. I'll never forget the fright in her eyes." I had to stop to wipe my tears. "Once I was out on the patio and spotted Genevieve standing in her window, looking helpless. A shadow of a man came up from behind and pulled her back. When I rushed inside, she was in bed ... alone. The nurses reported that no males, visitors or staff, had been in there."

Seeing the two detectives look at each other quizzically, I felt they still did not believe me. "There was a report made to the Director about this." They showed no acknowledgement. "There was a meeting. I was called into Wolfe's office to discuss this incident." Still, no flicker of recognition. Their blank faces waited to hear more. "Check with Wolfe!"

The brunette finally spoke up, "He's away on travel."

I had to laugh. "What happened to don't-leave-town-till-this-investigation-is-over?"

They pretended to chuckle but the redhead admitted, "That's only in the movies."

There was my opening. "Speaking of the investigation, how's it going?"

The redhead asked, "You'll treat what we tell you as confidential?"

"Of course, I might even be able to help you these last days while I'm here?"

The rat face eyeballed her partner before finally leveling with me. "There's something odd here. Genevieve didn't have a circle of relatives and friends who might've had a motive to kill her. We delved into her background and couldn't find one person who'd profit by her death. The way we figure it, the old gal might've been killed by someone inside the facility. Perhaps an employee she caught stealing or molesting patients ... maybe even her?"

The redhead interjected, "Which is why we'd be interested in what you see or hear."

"Did you check out all the employees?" I asked, crossing my fingers for Pat.

She nodded. "Rehabs are obligated by the Commonwealth to perform background investigations and use due diligence in their hiring."

"What did you find out about the two men who run this place?"

They looked at each other before the taller one said, "Wilder Wolfe and Kyle Marx are another story. Their credentials are from overseas and their backgrounds here are sketchy."

I asked, "Did they know each other before they came here?"

"No, Wolfe was brought on board about five years ago. Marx arrived three years later."

You have no other ideas why Genevieve was killed?"

The redhead said, "Only that the poor woman might have been killed by mistake."

I wondered if that theory was brought to their attention by Darlene, but I did not ask. My real curiosity concerned the security camera tape showing a man leaving the facility in my wheel chair the night of the murder. I held my tongue because I could not give away what Pat had told me. Instead I asked, "There's not one suspect?"

They shook their heads and I sensed they were telling the truth. The redhead gave me her card and asked me to call with any new detail. When they left, I drank the last of my cold coffee and knew what I had to do.

Thirty minutes later, hours before my allotted time with Beck, my hands were lightly pushing my walker up the hallway. Limping through the doorway, I saw familiar and new faces spread around the gym making valiant efforts to work through their pain. Some sat in wheel chairs, hurting and full of meds, trying hard to raise their arms. Others dragged their limbs, one foot in front of the other, along the parallel bars. The more advanced expended great amounts of energy pushing the machines. All worked hard in order to earn their ticket home.

The sudden roar of applause took me by surprise. I finally understood that my fellow residents' excitement was not specifically meant for me or my progress. They cheered to see that progress and healing was a possibility. Those who struggle, celebrate victories. I let go of the walker to clap and cheer their progress, their victories.

Darlene clapped from her wheelchair the longest. As usual, she was working out with Cheryl. I flopped into an empty chair next to her and they both grinned when Cheryl gave me hand weights. I fell into sync with Darlene and we began stretching our arms as we used to do together for so many weeks.

As we sped up our repetitions, the other patients increased their efforts to catch up to our rhythm. Cheryl stood up and called out to the patients, "This gym is rocking. Keep it UP!"

When we finally finished, sweaty and happy, Darlene and I wheeled toward the door. I hollered to Cheryl, "I'll return the chair on the way back." She waved okay and we left. It felt odd to be pushing the big wheels again, but fun. Darlene had her cigarette hanging from her lips as we cut through the cafeteria on our way to the patio.

Instead of stopping at the patio, Darlene kept going along the cement path. Since I had never been this far, wheeling down the winding path and circling the trees felt like an expedition. We rolled out of the tiny grove onto the far away parking lot. It was empty without cars this time of day. Knowing this was where Pat said the tunnel ended, I was curious to look around.

Darlene had already stopped to light her cigarette, allowing me to canvas the vacant blacktop until I found the door. I swung by it in the wheelchair still keeping my eye on Darlene. She loved to smoke and leaned back to enjoy every puff. I made a second pass by the exterior door of the secret tunnel, but saw nothing strange.

"Hey, come back. I got lots to tell ya." Darlene took a another drag and smiled as I pulled up next to her. Smoke was still streaming out of her nostrils as she asked, "Whaddaya think about the cops crawling around this joint?"

"They did a good job searching through our stuff the night of the murder. My wardrobe was ransacked." I feigned concern and asked, "I worried they'd find your switchblade?"

She fell back laughing, "Are you kidding me? I've had both my bar and my apartment tossed plenty by the law. Which is why I keep that silver beauty on my person at all times."

"Didn't the police ask you to empty your pockets the night of the murder?"

"Sure, but my blade wasn't in a pocket, or even in my clothes for that matter."

She made me curious. "Then how do you keep it on your person?"

Her smile widened."What's the one thing fat girls have that skinny girls will never get?"

I had to think about it. "All I come up with is fat. Skinny girls never get fat."

"Yep, fat. Luxurious ripples of flesh that were once comely love handles when I was more concerned with satisfaction than protection. Those soft crevices I selfishly kept for the probing hands of a lover. Now, those deep furrows offer hiding places for a smoke, a blunt, a hundred-dollar bill or my thin blade." She stopped to take a drag and laugh. "My hiding places will stand up to any warden's pat down."

While listening to her, it hit me that we had led very different lives. I wondered how I had I not deduced this before? Perhaps it was the pain meds fogging my brain. Or maybe, I was not playing detective when Darlene had befriended me. Now that I could see past her zany side, I suspected that Darlene lived on the dark side of morality. She may have even done time.

"The cops keep coming back, asking questions." I wanted to keep the conversation going.

"Awe hell, they haven't got a clue. They'll never figure out who got to Genevieve, but we know. Don't we." She turned to shine her toothless smile at me.

But this time, her sly ways came across as ominous and she began to frighten me. "Darlene, we cannot be sure it was Harold who mistook Genevieve for you?"

She put up her hand to stop my rationalizing. "I'm sure. And, you'll keep my secret."

"You didn't tell your suspicions to the police?"

"Hell NO! I don't want the cops snooping in my business. Besides, my boys are out looking for old Harold. They'll take good care of him."

Her directness left me lost for words. Finally, I was able to ask, "And if Harold is innocent? Won't you feel awful?"

Darlene lifted her cigarette and took another puff. Blowing smoke before looking over at me, she smiled. The hatred in her eyes sent shivers up my spine. "Harold is dead to me, whether he killed Genevieve or not. His life is over."

Later that evening, when Pat came in my room, we discussed this dilemma. She listened carefully and finally concluded, "We have no evidence that her boyfriend mistook Genevieve for Darlene and killed the wrong woman. That's Darlene's opinion. And, if she didn't tell her theory to the police, we're not responsible to pass along this rumor. Besides, good police work entails finding out who shared the room with the victim, or who slept in the bed prior to the victim."

Pat always had a way of putting the proper perspective on worrisome things. "You're right. From what I heard from the two detectives, it doesn't sound as if the county is practicing good police work. But, in their defense, how many murders do they get to investigate?"

"Who we should worry about is this Harold character and whether we should get the authorities to protect him?" She stopped and looked confused. "Meg, do we even know if there is a Harold? This could be cheap talk from a woman who acts like an Attention Whore."

"I've never met him? And if we tell the authorities, Darlene will deny everything if she's confronted by the law."

Pat winked. "Let's leave this sleeping dog lie for the time being."

Chapter Twenty-One

I was tired when Pat left my room to join the evening shift as they put up decorations for the big party. It felt good to get into bed and rest on the crisp sheets. My knee had already let me know that it was tired and my brain hurt from too many questions and not enough answers.

Since the Virginia heat and humidity had dropped after sunset, I opened the sliding window facing the front of the building. The balmy breeze flowed easily through the screen and brought a fresh floral scent reminding me that soon I would be going home to my own garden.

Although the new rules demanded that my door stay open during the night, all hallway lights were being dimmed. Twilight, as they called it, did not shine in my eyes.

Grabbing the remote, I clicked on Jimmy Kimmel and watched him work through his monologue. His silly take on world news always made me laugh. This night was no exception. He poked fun at all the politicians, the Hollywood crowd and showed a variety of pet clips that had been playing on YouTube. I felt my eyelids flutter. Sleep would not be far away.

Feeling light and slipping away from my body, my essence floated free from its physical restraints. This nocturnal journey, traveling away from the pain of my present day, was a dream flight taking me back to a place where my family was whole again. There was our old house. Standing at the backyard grille was my husband looking healthy again.

A younger, naive version of me stood in the kitchen looking happy while chopping lettuce and singing to an old tune. And baby-makes-three cooed to me from his highchair. Because I was the director of this illusionary scene, I willed my hand to smooth the baby's cheek and my dreaming self could almost feel his soft skin again.

This joy that I wanted to last forever came to an abrupt end and I was brought back. Something or someone had entered my safety zone and set off my internal alarm. I opened my eyes to a dark room. The timer had turned off the television and there was only the palest of light streaming from the hall. Without clear vision, I stayed still. Watching and listening, straining my eyes and ears, I waited. The sound of metal sliding along metal made my heart stop. The window was being opened all the way and I caught sight of a dark shadow trying to crawl inside.

My heart pounded in my throat from lack of oxygen. I slipped my hand across the sheet to the control panel on the bed rail. I was well practiced in knowing which button called for emergency assistance. When I hit it, the light on the wall flashed brilliant red and I could hear bells ringing at the Nurse's Station.

The hooded shadow now climbing out of the window turned and looked directly at me.

In that fight-or-flight second I had to decide: jump up and run or stay and fight? There was little choice for me. Surprisingly, the intruder climbed back out the window and ran.

Pat was the first to come running through the door. I pointed to the window. "Someone got in, but climbed back out!" She flew over to it and before I could argue, she climbed out of the window and disappeared into the night.

I had already dropped to the floor and was limping on my bare feet. By the time I got to the window, all I could see was Pat's shadow sprinting through the grass on her way to the frontage road that wound along the front of the building and down to the highway. Three CNAs blew in the door and circled around me. Together, we watched Pat cross the road.

She stopped before running into the grove of trees that ran parallel to the road and turned around. Shrugging her shoulders, Pat let us know that she lost sight of the intruder. When she started walking back, I turned around and explained to the girls what had happened. Distracted, I answered their questions. None of us heard when the car engine started up. When it was gunned, we all turned back to the window to look.

I pointed to the other side of the road now hidden in the dark. "The noise seems to be coming from over there."

While our eyes searched for the source, we spotted Pat walking up to cross the road. Seeing us in the window, she waved before stepping off the curb. When she was halfway across, a dark SUV came flying out from the shadows. Running without lights, it headed straight for her. Pat tried to jump back, but it was too late. The dark military-type vehicle swerved to the left, sideswiping her intentionally.

We watched helplessly as her body flew up looking like a rag doll. We all screamed her name until my ears hurt. As the hit-and-run driver sped up and passed by the window, one of the CNAs crawled out and ran to Pat now sprawled on the pavement. The other two ran out of the room, screaming for help.

Terrorized by both the intruder and what we had just witnessed, I stood alone ... shaking. Not able to take my eyes off my dear friend laying unconscious, I could not leave the window. Within seconds, sirens screamed from the highway below followed by a parade of flashing red lights winding up the road. A few seconds earlier and they would have passed the fleeing SUV. The quick response should have made me feel better, but knowing that I could not accompany Pat to the hospital pulled me into depression.

I watched two paramedics climb out and quickly take charge, relieving the CNA administering to my best friend. Pat must have been responsive as they quickly strapped on an oxygen mask. Waving off arriving police officers, the EMTs loaded Pat into the back of the ambulance and took off for the hospital.

Tears flowed as I watched the emergency vehicle speed away and when I turned around, the beautiful Asian night nurse was coming at me with a hypodermic. Before she had a chance to shoot me up, the room started to spin and the wooden floor flew up and hit me in my face.

When I woke up in my bed there were several strangers staring down at me. The night nurse was the first to smile and ask, "How are you feeling?"

"I'm fine. How long have I been out?"

The angel in white checked her watch. "About two hours."

Sitting up, I still felt woozy. "How's Pat? Have we heard?"

"Yes, she has a concussion and is full of bumps and bruises. Her right leg caught the worst of it. She has a fractured tibia and torn meniscus."

My mouth dropped as I repeated Pat's injuries, "Broken tibia and torn meniscus. Do you mean she has a broken leg?"

"Oh yes, she'll be laid up for weeks once she has surgery."

"But, she will survive it all and walk normal again?"

"That's the plan." She winked. "There's some officers here who want to talk with you."

Chapter Twenty-Two

As the county cops questioned me, I answered honestly and told them everything that had happened. I described how someone had pulled off the screen and got into my room through the window. Pat chased the suspect across the frontage road until she reached the grove. Surmising now that the perpetrator had circled back, we all saw Pat run down by that marauding SUV.

The two male detectives who I had never seen before dismissed the other officers in uniform and medical personnel who were present. The younger of the two began eye-balling my room. He was young enough to be tech savvy and I suspected that he was looking for surveillance devices.

The senior partner with snowy white hair reminded me of Steve Martin, the comedic actor. He smiled and spoke softly, trying to make a connection. "Meg, let's talk." Again there was the smile when he added, "Investigator to investigator. We know you and Pat Hannelly are licensed." He waited for my nod, but I did not give it to him. "You gotta admit how surprising it is that you're a patient here and your partner took a job here." Again, he waited for me to warm to his conclusion, but I stayed cool. "C'mon, you can tell me. You girls working a case here?"

I pulled up my pajama leg and pointed to the red scar running eight inches down my knee. "Take a look and see why I'm here. As for Pat, did you talk to her at the hospital?"

"There's no talking to Pat right now. The docs won't allow it."

"She'd be the only one who could tell you why she took this job. I've been off duty for weeks working only to rehabilitate. Most of the time I've been here, I wasn't able to walk."

"The younger policeman who shared the distinct stare of the dead actor, James Dean, stepped alongside his partner. "We appreciate that you're a legit patient, but why your partner's working here is a mystery?"

"She is a licensed CNA. Could it be that when I was sentenced to rot here for weeks that she wanted to keep an eye on me while making a few bucks? We are a start-up agency. It usually takes the two of us to work a job. I'm sure you gentlemen understand." I stopped to make my point by staring at them. "If you don't like any of my answers, you'll have to talk to her."

"Then tell us this, Ms. Hennessey." The cocky one threw back at me. "Why someone would climb in *your* window and why someone would run over *your* partner?"

"Tell me first, why would someone kill a poor old lady?" They looked sheepish. "Oh, you forgot that crime already. Or, has someone solved it?"

The senior cop put up his hand. "Calm down. We get the picture and we need your help. Can you at least give us a better description of the SUV?"

I switched gears. "There's an element that keeps coming back to me. As it sped below the street light, there was a reflection on a silver emblem. When it lit up under the street light, I tried to place it. All I keep thinking of is the symbol for water."

The senior man asked, "You mean h2o?"

I got excited. "Yes, h2o. That's it!"

Both policemen took in this new detail, until the younger one smirked. "I've got it. The Humvee 2 wears an H2 emblem!"

I smiled. "It's black with four doors. Shouldn't be hard to locate the registration."

They asked me to stay in touch and I accepted their cards. After they left, I laid my head back and tried to make some sense of what was going on, but all I came up with were questions. Who crawled into my window? Did he or she work alone or was a driver waiting outside? Why was Pat run down? Who killed Genevieve? Can I trust the details that Darlene keeps feeding me? Who's the ghost using the tunnel to disappear out of the building. Where's Wolfe and why haven't I seen Kyle lately?

It also hit me how Pat, and by extension me too, had been consorting with the Langley spooks. My stomach flipped thinking how hard Pat had been working to secure innocent stateside jobs for us from that ego maniac crowd notorious for being ruthless. They originated the game plan of throwing a fall guy under the bus. And that piece of intelligence had been whispered to me long ago by a dead soul who had worked beside them for years.

With Pat out of the picture, I also had a dark suspicion that Luc Raines or one of his henchmen would pay me a visit. A chill shivered across my shoulders at the thought of swimming alone in this fish bowl without the ability to leave until Dr. Saville released me. My appointment on Monday could not come soon enough.

I pulled out the cell phone and called Fairfax Hospital. The Information Desk reported that Pat Hannelly was sedated and resting in a room without a phone and would be kept there until her surgery. I left a thinking-of-you message and wondered if I should contact Danny, her son away at college? And while tossing that idea around, I fell into a dreamless sleep.

Hours later, my shoulder was shaken by a hand nudging me awake. Opening my eyes and ears, I heard a hammer pounding and saw Lyrie's beautiful smile. "If you don't make your breakfast choices now there won't be any food left." She pointed at the menu.

The hammering started up again and my eyes were drawn to a workman standing at the sliding window. It looked as if he was installing some kind of small devices.

"What's he doing over there?"

"Management ordered metal stoppers so the windows will only open a few inches."

I groaned, "We're losing our fresh air? Dammit, more restrictions!"

"I wouldn't think you would complain about new safety measures."

I waved off her remark. "What did you hear about last night?"

"Rumors are flying up and down the halls. We were warned to be careful around you."

I sat up. "What're you talking about?"

She fluffed my pillows. "Some say you might have caused all this trouble."

"Why the hell would anyone think that?"

She pretended to count the reasons on her fingers, "You complained that some man was trying to get under your covers and there were no men on the shift that night. You made a formal complaint that some man was molesting Genevieve and she got killed. You hit the panic button last night screaming that a man was climbing in your window and now Pat's in the hospital with broken bones."

My mind ran wild and I wanted to scream. After all, there was solid evidence for all of the accusations. Still, my voice of reason could see why my behavior might have seemed odd.

Lyrie looked sad. "I'm serious. You are on your own here. Mary and I are all you got. When we're not around ... you better not need any help."

"Good thing I'm going home soon." Lyrie nodded at my statement. "What can I do to get a cup of coffee," My pitiful quip brought Lyrie's happy smile back and she had my breakfast tray back in five minutes along with a copy of the Post.

After gobbling all the food, I moved to the chair with the paper and coffee. I quickly scanned the first page usually reserved for White House politics and news from The District. Pat's accident was on the second page, short and sweet. The police reporter had it listed as a hit-and-run with no mention of Pat chasing a man who had tried to crawl in my window.

As I read the article again, two tall men, wearing the white Roman collar and black suits of Catholic priests, stepped inside my room. They did not look holy as they took positions inside the door and stood as if they were on guard duty. Before I could say anything, a third appeared in the same priestly attire. As tall as the others, he came forward and pulled over a chair. Without saying a word, this handsome man with emerald eyes and sun-streaked hair sat in front of me.

While admiring his summer tan, I tried to remember when I had my last confession. Since this man did not have the uninterested eyes of a confessor, I wondered what he wanted?

He smiled. "Do you know why I'm here, Meg?"

"It's not to give me communion?"

He winked. "You know who I am?"

"I do." It could only be one person. "You're a friend of my partner."

"That's right."

"She delivered the information you wanted, correct?"

"Yes, and it's being investigated." He took my hand and put it in his, but it kept shaking.

"Why are you here?" I could hardly get out the words.

"I'm worried about both of you girls."

"That's kind of you."

"I feel responsible," his eyes looked penitent, "because I sent you here."

"We completed the tasks of our contract, correct?"

"Yes, but Pat was on board to continue the investigation."

"That's impossible now. You know where she is; you know what happened!" He nodded, but waited for my inevitable question. "What did you want Pat to do?"

He paused to squeeze my hand and look deep into my eyes. "There are evil people in this world. Do you agree?"

Without hesitation I nodded. "Yes, I do."

"There might be one or two right here, masquerading in this facility."

"Could be."

"Oh Meg," he whispered low, "what can we do about these demons?"

This man knew how to unlock the door to my rage. I sensed that he wanted to fire me up and hear my outcry for justice. And I gave it to him. "We're going to find out who they are and destroy them!" My hands flew up to my mouth to stop the tirade. How could I talk that way? Needing to explain I blurted out, "A woman who never hurt a soul got her neck slashed here and my friend who emptied bed pans to keep an eye on me got run down. I'm mad as hell!"

"I just came from the hospital." He gave me a friendly smile. "I'm mad as hell too. Pat did not deserve what happened to her." He pulled out a linen handkerchief as I started to blubber. "You and I are partners now. Agreed?" He dabbed my tears and I nodded. "You find out who these demons are and let me take care of the rest."

When he got to his feet, his priestly figure reminded me of the elegant actor Richard Chamberlain in THE THORN BIRDS.

"How can I contact you?" I needed to know before they left.

"Don't worry," he nodded to the two men still standing at the doorway, "we'll be close."

And like that, Luc Raines walked out the door.

My new course had been set in a few minutes with a few words by a man dressed up in disguise. I tried to clear my head to assemble some sort of plan. My first job was to get out of my room and hear what people were saying about last night.

I got dressed and pushed my walker into the hallway. The facility seemed empty as I made my way to the Nurse's Station. Passing the empty gym decorated with giant paper flowers hanging from the walls and ceilings, I remembered that it was Saturday, the day of the Bazaar. The workout equipment had been pushed back in case the party needed to come indoors.

Rounding the corner, I stopped at the Nurse's Station. The male nurse who I did not know was working it alone. He wore a funny paper hat and gave me a consoling smile. "Hey Ms. Hennessey, we haven't met before. I'm Tomas. Sorry to hear what happened."

"Thank you, Tomas. I got a whopping sedative last night and don't remember much of what happened." I lied. "What did we find out? Is there new information?"

Tomas was a nice looking Hispanic man with very dark eyes that stared at me, no doubt wondering whether to speak openly. He bent over the high desk and whispered, "The cops want to lock down Barrington Hall, but Kyle Marx won't hear of it. And when they demanded that he cancel the Bazaar, the Assistant Director called police headquarters and complained.

"Kyle's in charge now?" I was in shock.

"The Director's on travel. No one seems to know where or when he'll be back."

"Doesn't that seem strange?"

"We all wonder about it. Some think Wolfe might've been let go by The Board?"

"How do you like working for Kyle?"

"He leaves the professionals alone. I can't complain." Tomas looked away, anxious to change the subject, "How're you feeling today, any complaints?"

"Thank you, no." I switched the subject back, "How's Pat? Have you heard anything?"

"Hospital reports she's awake and alert. Surgery is planned for Monday."

"She was so brave last night, running after that bastard."

He smiled. "Brave or maybe a little loco? What she did is NOT in her job description."

I looked around at the empty corridors. "Where's everybody?"

"They're starting the celebration outside. You should join them."

I waved goodbye and continued to walk toward the cafeteria. Passing the patient rooms, I could see that they were empty too. All televisions and radios were off which added to the unusual quietness. Turning into the cafeteria, I was amazed to see the tables all decorated.

Steering my walker to the patio, the sound of singing reached out to me. When I got to the glass doors and looked out, I saw my fellow patients walking or riding in their various modes of transportation. A sea of smiling faces ran out to the front lawn and all the way to the road. Working the crowd were jugglers, magicians and clowns. An old-time barbershop quartet led voices in tunes from the last century. I pushed open the door and meandered into the crowd.

Chapter Twenty-Three

Walking into the gala was like stepping into a play land. My mood lifted seeing the patients laughing and having fun, free from pain and worry even for a little while. The staff members were in costume and had magically transformed from ogres to entertainers.

Booths were set up with a variety of sweet treats and carnival fare. Vendors and staff dressed like carneys sat at tables advertising their abilities to win at guessing games or Three-Card Monte. Next to them were the faithful from a variety of beliefs eager to minister to our spiritual needs. Travel and tour mongers advertised from a big booth while entertainment coupons were being hawked at another. There were hot dog stands next to cotton candy machines. Taco vendors cooking next to chicken fryers: all culinary delights that the facility's dietician had kept off limits.

My taste buds heightened by the variety of aromas reminding me of childhood pleasures. In particular, it was the smell of steaming frankfurters and all the fixings that dragged me to the Chicago hot dog stand. Pushing my walker, I fell in line behind Darlene's wheelchair without noticing that it was her. When she turned around with a cigarette dangling from her mouth, we both looked surprised.

Before Darlene could speak, a smoker's cough overtook her hello. Waiting for her to regain her breath, I bent down and gave her a hug. "It's good to see you."

Moving along in line, we commiserated about the joy of eating hot dogs with cold beer. She winked up at me. "My sons brought me a few iced drinks this morning before they left to open the bar." She pointed to a small cooler riding on her lap. "Let's go sit at a quiet table."

I purchased four hot dogs for us and followed her to an empty area on the front lawn where small tables and chairs awaited. It felt good to sit outside in the lush greenery to enjoy the sunshine and party atmosphere.

I opened the bag as Darlene pulled out two cardboard cups with lids wearing labels from a specialty coffee house. As she handed one to me, my fingers could feel the cold coming from inside. Before taking a bite of the hot dog, I threw back a long swallow of ice cold beer. Eager to taste the alcoholic content, I was not disappointed. Swallowing more, I enjoyed the calm feeling that beer always brought to me.

When I finally stopped gulping, I spotted Darlene gobbling her hot dog with one hand and slurping from her cup with the other. We both stopped to smile at each other as a big burp bounded out my mouth. Laughing, we continued to enjoy the fun food.

Picking up my second hot dog, I slowed down to look around. Many of the staff wore festive costumes with eye masks and wigs. Some were outfitted as cartoon characters while others were dressed like rock stars. I pointed out a few that I recognized, but Darlene did not seem to care. She nudged me, pointing out two more cups still in the cooler. We laughed like sneaky teenagers as she passed the second beers to us.

"Let's take this one slow," Darlene settled back in her wheelchair. Looking out at everyone enjoying the gala she sighed. "Geez, I almost forgot how sweet it is to have fun."

"We've been prisoners for weeks." The cell in my pocket began to play, DIXIE. Since I had never heard the ringtone on this new phone, it startled me. Excusing myself, I stepped away from the table. The melody was Pat's favorite and I was excited to talk to her.

Her voice sounded weak. "Hey partner, whatcha up to?"

"I'm so sorry, Pat. Your injuries are my fault." I could feel my eyes tearing.

"Oh, stop! I was out that window before you knew I was gone." She chuckled, "You know how I love to run."

"Indeed, I do," I recalled our foot races around the school track, "I've never beat you."

"Bet you can beat me now!" We laughed.

"What about your upcoming surgery ... are you okay with it?"

"Yeah," She sighed, "I'm looking forward to getting it over with and start healing."

"Doesn't that sound familiar?" I chided her. "Can you talk and tell me what happened?"

"Yeah, I'm alone. I gave that guy a good chase, was almost on him when he ran into the trees. He must have come around and slipped into his SUV."

"Tell me what he looked like?"

"At least six feet tall and lean, dark pants and long sleeve tee. He might have had very dark makeup on because I was right behind him under the street light and couldn't make out his features. Probably the same person in the gym who took your chair."

"Which would make him Genevieve's killer."

"Agreed, but do you have any idea why he would climbing in your window?"

A chill came over me in the eighty-degree heat. "Only one that makes sense."

"You've spotted him twice. Once in Genevieve's window and once in the gym." She gave me a few seconds to contemplate. "Perhaps you should leave that place before Monday, Meg?"

"Pat, I had a visitor today." I ignored her question.

"I sorta guessed you would. Did he talk you into working for him?"

"He didn't have to try very hard."

"Did you fall in love with him?"

I chuckled. "Not hardly! He and his companions presented themselves as priests."

Pat's full blown laugh sounded painful. "The perfect getup for a man who will be eternally unavailable. Would have loved to seen it. Bet he had you guessing?"

"At first, but the green eyes were a giveaway."

She sighed in resignation. "He's still a good contact for our business."

"That's right. And you and I promised to never mix pleasure with business."

"That's true," again her sad sigh. "Sometimes easier said than done."

Not knowing how to comfort her, I finally mumbled, "We sure know how to use clichés."

Without missing a beat she shot back, "Clichés always work when the truth hurts."

An awkward silence ensued. I finally said, "I'll call tonight and tell you all about the bizarre Bazaar."

"Go and have fun." I wished her well and gave her my love.

Walking back to Darlene, I saw her smoking yet another cigarette and nursing her brew. Anyone could see how much she missed her saloon life. I thought about my own father, who was most comfortable sitting at a bar, a man's bar, enjoying good conversation and a stiff drink.

As calm as I felt from drinking beer, my mind was still focused. I needed to get answers, but most of all I needed to question Darlene to find out the truth. Could it have been Harold who killed Genevieve by mistake? Or, does Darlene hate this man so much that she would rope him in to a murder charge just to see him rot in jail?

Darlene smiled up at me and I saw her curiosity. "Who was on the phone?"

"That was Pat, the poor CNA who got run over chasing that intruder."

Darlene's happy smile drooped. She almost looked ashamed. "That damn Harold!"

"Darlene, are you sure this is Harold breaking in here, murdering that poor woman?"

She got mad and practically jumped up from her chair. "Well, who else could it be?"

I sat at the table and said, "Tell me what the man looks like, or do you have a photo?"

"Nah, no photos. He shies away from cameras. Soon as I'd take one, he'd rip up the film." She dropped her smoked cigarette into the empty coffee cup and proceeded to light another. "Harold's tall, dark and handsome. Probably too handsome for me. I should've known better."

"When you say dark? Is Harold Indian dark, Arab dark or Black dark?"

"Harold is an Arab. Thought I told you? Came here from the explosive Middle East."

"Do you know which country?"

She shook her head. "We never talked politics. I was grateful he found me attractive."

"Did he attend school here or work here?"

"Yeah, he worked downstairs with me tending bar. I hired him as a bouncer first. One look from his beady eyes stopped any trouble before it got through the door."

"He must've given you references?"

Darlene began to smile. "You don't know anything about the bar business, do you?"

I had to laugh. "No. No, I sure don't. Sorry to have to ask, but how did you meet him?"

"He was a regular downstairs. Never heard anything bad about the guy. Everybody in the bar seemed to know him," she stopped to think, "and my bartenders told me how he helped with a couple of skirmishes. Harold knew how to get the instigators out the door."

"He must be a big guy?"

"Maybe six something, but all muscle. He's fast. Never saw anyone who could jump over a bar to knock heads like him." Her eyes softened. "I miss him and I hate that we're fighting."

"Any chance you two could make up, start over?"

She looked up and icicles formed in her eyes. "You ever been thrown down a staircase?"

I had to admit. "No, I have not and it would be hard for me to forget such a thing."

She shook her head. "I refuse to forget, especially when I know he's still after me."

"Your gut still says he's trying to kill you, but killed Genevieve by mistake?"

"I'm past thinking it was by mistake. I gotta think Harold realized the mix up, used the window scene to frighten me and came back to kill her to let me know what was coming to me."

"And you think it was Harold climbing in my window and running over the CNA?"

"Yep, he knows how to case a place and get information. He found out you and I hang together. Probably figures I've told you everything. You're lucky that your CNA got into your room so fast, or you could have gone the way of Genevieve."

"And he's the kind of guy who'd deliberately run down Pat?"

"Why would I be surprised about that?"

Feeling dizzy, I drank the entire second cup of beer and burped again. "Darlene, that's a stretch. Genevieve had been screaming for help the whole time she was here. To me, she was being harassed ... maybe molested even?"

"Molested? Nah, that's not Harold, but he could have been trying to scare me all along."

"What about the guy pulling down our covers during the night? He was a molester." She did not answer. "Bottom line, Darlene, if you think Harold is involved? Why not tell the police?"

"I cannot get the police involved." She yelled back at me. "You'll have to stay quiet and trust that I know what I'm doing." She reached into her pocket for her pack of cigarettes. I waited while she went through the light-up ritual and after she took her first drag, I asked again why she could not trust the investigators. She looked up from her smoke and for the first time, I saw fear in her eyes. I drew in my own breath when she whispered, "He knows where my grandkids live."

Chapter Twenty-Four

Darlene wheeled away from the table, saying she needed a nap. I watched her leave, knowing that I would have to keep her speculations secret from the police. Whether they were true or not, she believed that the tinniest of her loved ones were in danger. Were her sons chasing Harold, and would they kill if they caught him? I was left with more questions than answers.

Since I was scheduled to leave Barrington Hall in two days, I wanted to put Darlene's accusations out of my head in order to investigate the facts. For now, I decided to step away from Darlene's issues. Somehow, I felt the truth about them would show itself ... eventually.

Walking back to the festivities, I was drawn to the Fortune Teller tent. A nice looking man, casually dressed in tee and jeans, sat at a tiny table wearing a no-name ball cap over dark sunglasses. His appearance was not like the typical seer. Head down, he kept shuffling his deck of playing cards, making him look more like a casino dealer.

When I sat across from him, he slid the deck across to me. "Shuffle three times and cut."

It had been a long time since I had held cards. The deck felt hot, full of energy from his hands. I shuffled and folded the cards back.

He smiled. "Shuffling cards is a skill that is never forgotten."

"Like riding a bike." I answered.

After the second shuffle, I made the final cut. Looking over at the man now studying me, I wondered if this ritual, traditionally requested by all card readers, gave them time to tap into our psyches and observe our body language.

While trying to get a better look at the man who kept his head low, I sensed something familiar. He kept his voice soft as he instructed me to spread out a circle of four cards with a fifth in the middle, all facing down. When I finished, he took the remaining deck and put it to the side.

Looking closely at the configuration, he took a few moments to study the cards. Finally, he explained. "Black indicates dark days and red illuminates better times."

I suddenly felt ill at ease and squirmed in the squeaky fold-up chair.

Pointing to the top card he said, "This card represents your recent past." Flipping it over, we both looked down at the King of Spades. A low whistle flowed out of his mouth. "The strong king in your life recently died after fighting a long, hard battle." He waited.

I did not respond, but my eyes would not move off the mustached king holding a sword.

"Do you want me to go on?"

When I nodded, he tapped the next card. "This position represents the present." He turned over the Ace of Spades and said, "Death is still around you."

"When do I get to hear good things?"

"There's never any guarantees." His well manicured finger pointed to the third card. "Here is your future." He flipped it over and I smiled. "Ah, there's a possibility of new love!"

I was glad to see the Queen of Hearts holding out her posies.

"The fourth card is your wish. If you haven't already made one, now's the time."

"Oh, I made a wish." And thought again how both, Pat and I, needed to get on our feet.

He turned over the fourth card and we stared at the Queen of Diamonds. When he remained quiet I asked, "What's wrong?"

"Red is positive. Your wish will come true." His tone did not sound convincing.

"And that's a good thing, right?"

"Yes, but it looks as if another female will share in your wish."

I refused to explain and left him in the dark as to the truth of what he foretold. He waited for an explanation, but I pushed him forward. "What about the card in the middle?"

"Here's where everything can change. The center card reveals whether the readings have been deceptive. Red means truth. Black means it was all lies."

As he moved to the last card, I shut my eyes until I heard him chuckle.

"I've never seen the cards be so honest." His easy manner assured me that I could open my eyes. When I looked, he was holding up the bright red Ace of Hearts. We laughed at the incredible reading and when I tried to give him money, he refused it. "Enjoy the rest of the day."

I left the table and strolled into the crowd, passing the hula girls swaying their hips and passing out leis. A small stage had been set up and an Elvis impersonator was crooning the dead singer's hits into a microphone. Everyone gathered around and sang along. The performer kept holding out his mic to the audience, picking up the happy voices that remembered the decades old lyrics. As I looked around, I spotted two others dressed as Elvis and had to chuckle.

Following the rich aromas in the air, I found the candy trailer that had been pulled up on the grass. There was my favorite: homemade fudge with walnuts. Ordering two small pieces, I was in heaven. It was not long before I began to lose my energy. The ache in my knee told me that it was time to go back to my room and rest my leg.

Wending my way back along the patio, I saw the crowd moving further out on the front lawn where more musical acts were playing on a new stage erected near the frontage road. Out of habit, I hit the disabled button at the cafeteria entrance, but walked through the automatic door opening. Reentering to the building was like stepping into a vacuum: no sound, no signs of life.

For no reason my heart began to race, as I walked along the hallway toward the Nurse's Station. I laid it off to the rich caffeine in the fudge. Rounding the corner, I was relieved the see Tomas still sitting behind the raised station. He looked up and asked, "How's the party going?"

"Barrington Hall should be proud of what they have accomplished today. Everyone's out there dancing and singing," I smiled sincerely.

"Why aren't you out there?"

And that's when the thought hit me that this would be the perfect time to snoop. "You're right, Tomas. I'm going to freshen up and get right back out there."

"Good. They're planning a beautiful outdoor feast at sunset. You won't want to miss it."

My footsteps sped up as I made my way back to my room. Pulling out the duffel bag hiding inside my wardrobe, I surveyed the few tools Pat had brought when I first arrived. As if hit by bolt of lightning, I was struck with what had taken place since that night.

Changing my clothes to dark jeans and long-sleeve black tee, my heartbeat raced even more. I stashed both phones brought by Pat, the replacement for my lost cell and the Satellite phone sent by Luc Raines, along with the penlight in my pants pockets. I quickly wrapped the tip of the sharp nail file in tissues so it would not stick my own flesh while pocketed.

As I headed for the door, I could have sworn I heard the sound of a small animal running around in the corridor. Walking out the door, there it was again: the scampering of tiny paws. I looked both ways, but saw nothing. Heading back towards the Nurse's Station, I doubted my sense of hearing and blamed my stuffy nose for my lack of audible range.

Tomas looked up and smiled again. "Don't you look nice. Where's your walker?"

"My first practice run without it."

Tomas, being a dutiful nurse, quickly checked my progress report and smiled. "Yes, you are ready to go it on your own. Do be careful. You don't want to fall again."

I nodded and laughed. "You didn't happen to hear little paws running around, did you?"

He put down his pen. "Don't tell me that crazy animal's out again."

"What crazy animal?"

"The staff and guests brought in a few of their pets to visit with the patients when the party's over. You know, stroking cats and petting dogs can be very calming. I've got them corralled in the Shower Room, but there's one pesky fella that keeps getting out." He laughed. "And if he's loose again, that bad boy will have a few minutes of freedom cause I can't leave the station right now."

Standing there, looking up at Tomas, we both laughed until a tiny silver streak flew by and he called out, "Get back here!" Looking helpless, Tomas shook his head.

A sinking feeling brought me back to that night in Georgetown, but. I returned to my information gathering, "Is Kyle Marx here today?"

"I heard staff saying that Assistant Marx would be in costume today."

"Oh that sounds exciting. Do you know which character he's dressed up as?"

"No. He likes to play surprises and only shows his face at the end of the party."

"That must be fun." I waited a couple seconds before asking, "Tomas, who owns Silver?"

His expression went blank. "I'm not sure. The dog's been coming here for awhile, but I've never met his owner to be truthful. Why? Do you know that little rascal?"

"Figured that little guy running around would be named Silver. He's so cute and spunky."

The sound of nails sliding across the polished floor turned our heads. Now running in the opposite hallway, Silver flew by. Tomas tossed his pen midair and looked exasperated. "That stinker's headed for the staircase."

"I've got nothing to do. I'll follow after him."

When I stepped away, Tomas stopped me. "You can't keep up with that dog. Don't worry, he won't get to the second or third floors. They're locked tight. No one's in the basement today so Silver can't get in trouble."

Chapter Twenty-Five

Waving a casual goodbye to Tomas, I started down the corridor. Once I was out of sight, I sped up and wended my way to the staircase where I stopped to listen. Silence. Where was that dog?

Grabbing the banister, I went down the stairs ... one step at a time. The bottom of the staircase opened into the basement's main hall, crossing in front of the elevators. I stood there and could see even by the dim light that all offices were empty and no doubt locked. Still, I walked slowly and tried each door. Both the Director and Beauty Shop's handles would not turn. I peeked through the glass of the Security Office. It was empty and their door was locked.

As Security's wall monitors flipped through the camera shots, I tilted my head to watch. The inside views showed how empty the facility was while the outside surveillance kept moving back and forth across the crowd. I watched how everyone out there moved further up the front lawns to enjoy the entertainers who were setting up to work the crowd. The patio and back of the building looked deserted.

Although I searched every shot as it flew by for security uniforms, they were nowhere to be seen. I wondered if perhaps the guards were also in costume mixing with the vendors, clowns and impersonators.

Something distracted me. Turning around, I saw nothing. Still, I did not feel alone. And when I looked down and saw Silver sniffing at my ankle, I wondered if he remembered me? Looking into his shiny black eyes, I bent down and petted his head. "Silver! You sly dog, where have you been hiding?"

He looked up at me as if he understood. Instead of barking, he jettisoned around the corner and I sensed that he actually wanted to show me where he had been hiding.

Following him around the corner and turning again at the next hallway, I should have been able to spot the dog. But, Silver was not there waiting for me. What I did see was the open door to Base A and I stopped. That place still frightened me. It took me a few seconds to gather my wits and review the reason why I was down there: to search for Silver was what Tomas would say. Pat would say I was on the job, gathering intelligence.

I crept close to the wall like a mouse until I got to the open doorway.

My hand reached up to the chain around my neck and I felt relieved that the copied door key that Pat had given me was still there even though I did not need it. Taking small steps toward the open entry, my good sense resisted going inside. The thought of the door being slammed shut behind me brought shivers to my spine.

Stepping around the door still standing open, I peeked into the dark gym. There was only minimal light behind me and no light in front of me. While my mind argued whether to go forward or retreat? I decided to close the door and walk away, but when I reached out to do that, I heard a faint squeal. Listening, I heard it again. Not a human cry shouting out for help, but an animal's response to pain.

My gut warned me that even though I had heard the cry for help coming from Base A, it could have come from inside the tunnel and no doubt originated from Silver. That damn dog! He had most likely gotten hurt by smacking his rear end into a pile of beat-up gym equipment. That is what I told myself as I left the door open behind me and made my way into the darkness.

Pulling out the penlight, I watched the tiny beam travel far ahead of me. I used it to scan the area still piled high with boxes to the right, but there was no movement ... no sign of Silver. When he squealed again, I could tell that his cry came from the back area straight ahead of me.

Traveling the narrow path that wound around piles of stored equipment, I walked deeper into the old gym until my head began to spin. Feeling disoriented, I stopped to get my bearings and that was when I heard the hall door slamming shut. My worst nightmare had just come true.

I turned off the penlight to wait and listen. I could only hope that this episode would be a repeat and that the door was merely closed by the guard to secure the old gym.

My prayers were not answered. Heavy footsteps confirmed that I was no longer alone.

Gripped by fear, I put my hand over my mouth to stop from screaming. By the sound of movement behind me, the intruder knew his way around without a flashlight. One set of footsteps meant that my tracker was operating alone.

His silence convinced me that he was not on a mercy mission to find the stray dog or a lost patient. My gut told me that this person was on the hunt, but I hoped it was not for the person holding her breath and afraid to move.

Orders from the survival part of my brain shouted out like a drill sergeant. I reached out in the dark and began to take baby steps. Feeling my way, I tried to remember this area. It was difficult since I had only been here once. Finally, a map appeared in my head and I remembered the dangerously narrow path curving around mounds of rusty metal. If I jiggled the wrong way, and my body fell into any one of them, I could be seriously hurt ... again.

My black gym shoes bought for stealth, kept silent as I managed to make my way. After several steps, I reached the small clearing in the vicinity of the tunnel opening. Tiptoeing forward like a blindfolded kid playing pin-the-tail-on-the-donkey, I could not find the metal cabinet where I expected it to be located. I stood frozen in the dark and heard my pursuer sneaking his way along the same path and would soon find me. Sweating from every pore, I felt a light breeze pass over me and knew the tunnel entrance was open.

I moved forward until the tips of my fingers found the edge of the tunnel door ... standing wide open. Staring blindly into the dark opening, I could hear Silver's soft moaning from deep inside. My stomach churned, but when the dog cried out again, I knew he had to be hurt or at the very least frightened.

My remembrance of the tunnel came back easier because I had already navigated the passageway in the blind. Pulling the door closed behind me, I turned on the penlight. The tiny beam could hardly break through the darkness. Still, I could see to where the path made a sharp turn which was where I suspected that the dog may have gotten hurt. I turned off the light, willing myself to go forward. Moving along, I threw off my fears in order to find Silver.

Something made me stop?

I stood and listened.

The tunnel door behind me was opening.

Chapter Twenty-Six

Shoving the penlight into my pants pocket, I began my attempt at the long dash to the end of the tunnel. My fingertips kept touching the walls to guide me as I hippity-hopped on my newly reconstructed knee. I lengthened my stride, hoping not to do any damage to the progress I had made so far. All the while, I thought about grabbing the dog and making it to the end door.

Forgetting about the turn, I almost ran into the brick wall ... again. I worked my way around it and realized that I had not heard from Silver in awhile. A few steps more and my foot tripped, but I caught my balance. Something was on the floor. When I bent down and felt around my hand found a tiny paw. I could feel the outline of a dog, but there was no movement except for shallow breathing. Silver was out cold.

I picked up Silver and held his listless body. Like a baby, he laid his head on my left shoulder. The smell of blood was strong and when I searched his coat, I felt stickiness on my fingers. Silver was bleeding from his underbelly and panting with pain. His heavy breathing ramped up to snorting. His moans and groans were so loud that they began to resonate through the tunnel. I held him close, trying to soothe him before his noisemaking got us both killed.

I picked up my journey and was now in the unfamiliar part of the tunnel. While Pat did say that there were two cutoffs from a crossroad up ahead and that she surmised that they went to the main kitchen and laundry, she did not tell me where it intersected. Keeping my left hand around the dog and my right hand touching the wall, I took a few steps and stopped to listen. When there were no footsteps coming from behind, I pulled out the tiny penlight. It showed the crossway several yards ahead, but the tunnel kept going straight past it without obstacles.

A loud *SLAM* from behind made me turn and point the light. My heart stopped. The beam shined on an extremely large pair of pink oxfords. I could not move. My eyes were mesmerized by the circus character now rising from what I supposed was the fall against the wall. I watched him get to his feet in those floppy shoes until a tall clown stood up dressed up in an oversized pink and black checkered suit. His greasepaint face made up like a sad clown looked sweaty. The brown eye circles and oversized lips were slipping down to his chin. My observation had only taken a second or two, but it seemed like hours.

As the clown rubbed his eyes against my tiny beam, I sensed that this was not someone sent to entertain me. I clicked off the light and before it was completely dark, I turned and ran. The dog stayed still in my arm with his head on my shoulder. The thought of throwing Silver down to trip the scary jester was a thought, but I could not do it even to save myself.

Making headway, I felt a change of air flow as I ran past the crossway leading to the other tunnel. Hoping that I was gaining distance, I sped up. Still the sound of floppy shoes, slapping on the cement behind me kept getting louder.

Trying to think ahead, I remembered Pat explaining how there was a bolted door up ahead that led to the parking lot. In that second, I felt a tug on my hair. Something was pulling at the back of my head. Without stopping, I clicked the penlight and pointed the light over my left shoulder. The spot lit up a demented joker face. Except now the rubber nose was dislodged and dangling over a menacing smile.

Seeing its white glove reaching out to grab more of me, I could not control the hellish shriek that roared up from my toes. The bizarre clown, breathing down my neck, appeared more frightening to me than any monster from my childhood nightmares.

Sensing my own mortality, I let out another shrill scream but somehow kept my light pointed in his eyes. Scream after scream erupted from me until suddenly the dog came to and began howling along with me. Our screaming duet made my ears hurt, but the flapping sound of clown shoes kept coming.

When both white-gloved hands tried to grab my shoulders, Silver turned in my arm. With his front paws up on my shoulder and my arm clutching his middle, the dog began to snap at our pursuer. Although this slowed the clown's attacks from the rear, we were still doomed. There was no way that I could outrun the long strides of this crazy clown. All the while, I kept wondering how in the hell I was going to explain this to Pat?

The dog began to lurch off my shoulder, aiming his snout for that red rubber ball dangling off the clown's exposed nose. Silver's second try was on target. He bit down and pulled off the red rubber ball. When it fell down, the dog got mad and more determined. He snapped at the clown's face again. This time his Pit Bull jaws bit down on the clown's nose. When Silver pulled back, I could hear the dog chomping and knew that he drew more than blood.

Now, it was our attacker's turn to yell out in agony. The sound of his cries weakened as we distanced ourselves. Never did I look back, nor did I feel sorry for his injury. I did wonder if Silver had been trained to bite for fresh meat or if it was a deep desire embedded in his genes.

I pointed the penlight ahead and saw the exit door. Since I could no longer hear clown feet chasing behind us, I had time to stop and throw back the bolt. Pulling open the metal door, I wondered what waited beyond?

Chapter Twenty-Seven

I had no sooner stepped out of the tunnel and into the parking lot when one of the phones in my pants pocket began to pulse. Pulling out both, I could see that the call was coming from the satellite phone with a dedicated line to Luc Raines. What would be making him call?

My arm was killing me and I wanted to set Silver down, but I kept him close because he was either sleeping again or passed out. While never losing sight of the tunnel door, I walked into the tree line for cover. My voice was shaking when I answered, "Hello?"

The male caller did not announce himself. Instead, there was a whisper. "Who is this?"

"Who is *this*?"

"Meg, is that you? Are you safe?" I recognized his well educated voice and tears of self pity welled ready to bubble over. Both legs hurt so bad that I slid my backside down the nearest tree until my bottom rested on the grass. I needed to sit down before I fell down.

"No, I'm not safe!"

"Where are you?"

"I just made a run for my life." I stopped because I did not want to tell about the tunnel.

"Listen to me. I have two men on the grounds. They're in disguise and they're searching for you right now. Please let me get their assistance to you."

"Disguises? What sort of disguises?"

"One's a rock 'n' roll impersonator and the other's a psychic. Have you seen them?"

"They're not clowns?"

"Why do you ask?" His voice dropped low. "Have you run up against a clown?"

My head was buzzing and I was not sure whether I should divulge my experience with the clown in the tunnel. I did not know what was safe to tell anyone anymore and was defensive.

"Please don't pussy-foot with me, Luc Raines. "

He chuckled, "Strange choice of words, but I will be straight with you."

"I would appreciate it."

"Are you outside of the building in a safe place?"

"Yes, I am outside. Unknown whether it's safe or not."

"It seems a male resident from the Third Floor escaped ... again."

"How did he escape from the mental ward?"

"Management's been keeping this dirty little secret even from the police ... until today. Seems this guy's a master of disguise. He sneaks off the floor somehow and must have a hiding place somewhere in the building. They usually spot him wandering outside, but no one knows how he's getting in and out of the facility."

"I think he dropped in on me one night. Is this escapee still on the prowl?"

"Yes, they think he got into the entertainers' wardrobe and dressed himself as a clown."

"Of course he did. I know this because a clown just chased me through the basement."

"I'll alert my men. Where did you leave this clown?"

"In Base A, the old gym. He'll be nursing a bloody nose ... what's left of it." I began to giggle from exhaustion and exhilaration.

"Do you want to talk to me about how this happened?"

"No. I just want to go back to my room."

"You can't do that. Please let my men find you?"

"If this mental patient is captured, what else is there for me to worry about?"

"Some woman there reported seeing her ex-boyfriend on the grounds, who may or may not be the killer of that poor lady. Do you know anything about that?"

"Oh yeah," I sighed, "that would be Darlene."

"Do you know Darlene or her boyfriend?"

"I know Darlene and I've heard of Harold."

"So that would be a problem for you. There's the missing Director. Have you seen him?"

"No, just heard a staff member say today that Wolfe's on travel."

"You think that's his real name, Wilder Wolfe?"

"You're asking me? Your agency has the global data bases to verify it."

"True. We'll follow up. And, what about the wily Kyle Marx?"

"He's supposedly on the grounds in costume. Why do you ask about him?"

"Marx has came up with some alias names that he likes to use."

"How'd he get through the facility's background check?"

"Like you said, it wouldn't be as thorough as ours." He laughed.

"What's Kyle accused of doing?"

"He's been associated with some kinky business ventures."

"And now he's working here?"

"That's why we want to talk to Wolfe."

All the while I had been on the phone, my free hand kept petting Silver to check his wounds. The scrapes on his underbelly were not deep and had already become crusty.

"Meg, are you still there?"

"Yes." I took a breath before I asked, "Would you tell me about the name, Mortez?"

"No!" He snapped back. "You don't have a need to know."

"But, that's what this mission is all about ... finding Mortez?"

"You're tasked with information gathering. Nothing more! You understand?"

Feeling dressed down and left out of the loop, I stayed quiet. How a handsome and intelligent man like Luc Raines could switch from amiable to caustic between sentences was beyond me. Mad, I determined to distance myself from any assistance offered by him or his henchmen. I would get back to my room, pack up my stuff and make my exit. The hell with Dr. Saville's release. I decided to sign myself out today and get the hell out of there!

"I hear you breathing." Luc chuckled into the phone. "I suspect that Meg is mad at me and quietly plotting revenge?"

I could not help but chuckle myself. "You have no idea what I've just been through."

"Why don't you tell me?" His voice softened.

"No!" I screamed into the phone. "Because YOU do not have a need to know!"

He burst into laughter. "Touche' and might I say that I did indeed have that coming."

My jaws tightened, my teeth ground together. I did NOT want to share his laughter. Instead, I spit into the phone. "You are an arrogant bastard!"

"Oh, oh! Tough girl, huh?" His humorous tone sounded smug again.

And that was when I hit the off button and shoved the cell back in my pocket. When it began to pulse again, I did not answer. I would work my plan without the aid of Luc Raines.

I was surprised to look down and see that the dog was sleeping in my lap. Giving him a few more minutes of rest, I laid my own head back against the tree and watched the sun setting low in the sky. Music from the front lawn played happy tunes and life seemed normal again. I could almost push the tunnel experience out of my head now that I knew that my pursuer was a known escapee and would certainly be captured when he went for medical assistance.

I also had my answer about who had come into my room that night under the pretense of wanting to change my diaper. Still, why would the escapee who must have been using the tunnel to get around kill Genevieve? That did not make sense.

And now, Darlene reported seeing Harold here. I wonder what she told the authorities?

Pat and I would no doubt never hear about the unfinished intrigue between the mysterious Mortez and the man that I now planned never to work for again!

Chapter Twenty-Eight

I awoke to sloppy kisses and a small tongue licking my lips. More than that, I felt tiny things crawling across my face. It was difficult to open my eyes. When I was finally able to see, I jumped to my feet and let Silver slip off my lap.

Standing back, I saw tiny red ants marching up and down the tree. Looking down, I saw ants crawling up and down me. Involuntarily, I went into an Indian dance. Rocking back and forth one foot to the other. My hands kept slapping at the dots racing across my face. I needed to get the creepy things out of my hair. Bending over and shaking my head, I could see the tiny things dropping to the ground.

All the while, Silver hopped on his hind legs snapping at the bugs as they fell off me. The silly animal was catching them in his mouth and eating them.

When I had brushed off the army of what I could now see were fire ants, there were still those regrouping inside my clothes. The war dance started up again, but this time as I did it my hands worked feverishly to tear off my outer clothing. Seeing clusters swarming at my belly button, I used my tee to brush them off while screaming at Silver for licking them off the ground. As I pulled off my bra and panties, I knew that I looked crazier than the dog. Now butt naked, I beat my clothes against my legs to make sure there were no insects waiting for me. Satisfied, I put on my underwear and caught my breath.

Silver began to act up. Running in circles, he chased his tail. I bent down and reprimanded him, "Serves you right for slurping up all those biting insects."

My vision suddenly narrowed and I felt faint. Reaching up to my face, I felt my cheeks beginning to swell. "The damn ant bites!" An allergy attack was coming on, but all of that was forgotten when I heard the tunnel door swing open.

Bending low to hide, I grabbed the dog and stroked his snout to keep him calm. We waited quietly, not knowing what to expect. I worried that it might be the ugly clown and hoped that I had not made a foolish presumption that the mental patient had been captured by now.

When Elvis Presley stepped out in the famous white outfit created for his Vegas comeback, I was curious to know if it might be one of Luc's boys searching for me. Still mad and not ready to trust anyone, I dropped low to the ground and pulled the dog close. Using my free hand, I rubbed low on Silver's belly ... the way to every males' submission.

Silver did not make a sound even when Elvis called out to him by name.

I rubbed even faster to keep him under control. And when the call to Silver rang out again, I recognized the voice. It was Silver's master from that night in Georgetown.

How could that be? I had suspected that it was Luc Raines who had sent the money and order to check on that Georgetown address. But would he have hired us to spy on one of his trusted men? No! He had people inside Langley to do that for him. Therefore, this rock 'n' roll impersonator could not be one of Luc Raines' boys. And if that was true, who in the hell was he?

When Elvis reentered the tunnel, I could only assume that he would bolt the door from the inside, which ended my ability to reenter through the tunnel. It did not matter. What did matter was Silver's master. Who was he and what was he doing here dressed up as Elvis?

I could not get that voice out of my head and kept trying to connect it to any other I had heard inside Barrington Hall.

Red and blue strobes of light flashing across the sky caught my attention. The intermittent beams, bouncing off the rolling clouds, created a surreal laser show. All I wanted to do was lay on the ground and watch it because my head hurt. When I realized that emergency vehicles were driving up from Georgetown Pike, I was not too alarmed. Police? Fire? Ambulances? Any of them could be winding up the private road to Barrington Hall at any time of the day or night. More of a curiosity was their silent approach of not using their sirens?

The silent coming of authority made me kinda feel uneasy. And for the first time, I could hear the pounding of the Potomac River descending the cliffs of Great Falls. The distant sound was musically serene. No doubt, the calming resonance had added to my falling into such a deep sleep before. Looking back at the parking lot, I also questioned how all the parked cars that had previously been there were able to start up and pull away without waking me?

Still feeling anxious over my loss of time, I realized that it was dark. Time to go inside.

There was a far-off sound of people talking excitedly coming from the side of the building. I listened to the distant voices and wondered why they sounded distraught? When the faces of Mary and Lyrie appeared, I hardly had the strength to wave let alone pick up my head.

They took off running ahead of Tomas and the others who strangely appeared irate.

Mary yelled, "Here she is ... we found her." Why did this not sound like joyful news?

Lyrie broke out of the pack and rushed to me. Not waiting to hear what I had to say, she bent down close to my ear and whispered through her teeth. Sounding accusatory, she scolded me. "Where have you been all afternoon and where are your clothes?"

I growled back, "I've been chasing that damn dog when I got attacked by fire ants."

"There's no fire ants in Virginia." She looked around. "What damn dog?"

When I followed her eyes, I saw that Silver was nowhere in sight. "Damn runaway!"

As the group was nearing, Lyrie struggled to dress me and whispered, "Are you okay?"

"Sure. Why wouldn't I be?" I whispered back and looked into her eyes.

"You've got a problem." She rolled back her eyes.

Looking over Lyrie's shoulder, I could see the strange stares approaching in the twilight. Worse, I did not like the way Tomas kept his hand behind his back. I struggled to my feet and backed away. Lyrie stood motionless, watching me as I moved further into the grove. I took one last look around for Silver, but that damn dog was smart and had already made his escape.

Seeing their menacing expressions getting closer, I turned and ran as my head kept spinning. How could all the good people, who I thought were my friends, be chasing me? And where was that damn dog?

I tried to sprint around trees, big and small, while jumping over bushes and dead branches. Like Frankenstein being chased by the villagers, I ran dragging my leg. How far could get before my knee would give out is all I kept asking myself. For a second, I felt that I might be able to outrun them. And I stayed confident until my right foot did not clear a log. When my body went down, I got the wind knocked out of me and laid on the ground ... panting.

When they caught up, I reached out for help. Instead of trying to get me to my feet, Mary and Lyrie held my arms down. Tomas stood over me wearing an angry smile of triumph. When his hand came forward, I could faintly make out the syringe. But, I felt it when he pushed the needle into my arm.

I screamed out, "What are you doing?"

Tomas dropped his fake smile. "It's for your own good, Ms. Hennessey."

"We've been worried about you." Mary's syrupy words did not sound sincere to me. Bending down, she took a good look at me and pulled back immediately. "Her face! She's full of bug bites." She acted like she was mad at me. "Did you take drugs? Or, try to kill yourself?"

My mind began to fade, but I heard Lyrie trying to explain something to me. "Please understand. When you disappeared, we had to call the authorities. After all, Dr. Saville did have you listed as a depressed patient."

Mary whispered to the others, "Such a shame. She was scheduled to go home Monday."

Two male CNAs, pushed their way through the feet standing around me. Kneeling down, they were holding a canvas jacket with dangling leather straps and metal locks. The two men rolled me over on my back and I knew that straight jacket was going to lock me up.

"Where are you taking me?" My arms kept pulling inside the sleeves. When they secured my wrists behind my back, a slow scream worked its way up my throat. Losing control, there was no way to stop it and I belted out a high octave that only a diva singing in Italian could hit.

Turning me over again, I began kicking. Although it hurt my knee to lash out, I got a few strikes in before they lifted me onto the gurney. When they tied my shoulders and ankles down, I kept shouting. "You've got it all wrong. Listen to me!"

Two county cops in uniform pushed through the small group and pointed their flashlights into my face. It did not matter. I called them filthy names. Their hard eyes stared down at me with disgust and I would have screamed more, but a wad of gauze was shoved into my mouth.

The CNAs led the trip back into the building and the chaotic crowd ran alongside me. Moving back through the trees and along the parking lot, I tried to lift my head and point to the tunnel door. No one paid attention; no one stopped to investigate. The team carrying me acted as if they were on a rescue. When in fact, it was that poor dog that deserved the gurney ride. Silver had open wounds and bugs eating out his insides ... not me?

Rolling through Barrington Hall's front door, I kept trying to sit up. When we stopped at the Nurse's Station, I tried to stay calm so they would take the gauze out of my mouth and let me speak. No chance, they talked over me, around me, behind me. Even Angela, my favorite nurse, kept her eyes away from mine. No one in that huddle acknowledged me.

It was Tomas who made quick notes on my chart. It was Tomas who handed that same chart to the male CNAs. It was Tomas who gave the order. "Take her to the THIRD FLOOR!"

The two cops tried to follow us into the elevator, but Angela called after them. "Sorry, officers, you can't go up there. It's restricted."

One of them rejected her order, "We need to speak with her?"

"That's impossible tonight." She answered in her angelic voice.

Tomas added, "Besides, she'll be unconscious in a few minutes."

When the elevator doors slammed shut, I cringed. As the elevator doors slid open, I could hear the chaos and smell the stench of the insanity. Welcome to hell on earth, I thought as they wheeled me to the place that had been waiting for my arrival all along.

HIDING PLACES AT BARRINGTON HALL

Chapter Twenty-Nine

Tomas was not lying. Unconscious sleep overtook me before my chart was handed over to my new jailors. The chemically induced empty state of mind was difficult to pull away from and I wondered how long I had been out. Minutes passed by as I watched the rays of sun shining across the ceiling from the tiny window. When my eyes finally opened wide, I could see that my body was now clothed in a hospital gown and covered with a thin blanket. My wrists and ankles were strapped down to the sides of the bed.

All the walls were covered with thick white pads and the floor was tiled in a black and white pattern. The metal door had a small window and I stared at it until eyes looked back at me.

A stranger in a nurse's uniform unlocked the door, walked in and looked around. "How are you feeling today?" Her voice was not friendly, only matter-of-fact.

"Fine, but I need to talk to the police. Two female investigators that visited me. They're the ones I need to speak with and soon." I was prattling, but I could not help it.

The tall woman came over and eyed the straps, making sure my hands and legs were still secured. Looking satisfied, she moved closer until I could get a look at her name tag: Sarah.

Holding back my panic, I calmly asked how long I had been on the Third Floor? Nurse Sarah pulled down the stethoscope hanging from her neck and began listening to my heart and lungs. She remained silent and I figured that her lack of interaction had to be a test. A test that I was determined to pass. I kept smiling, but cut out the chatter.

I tried to stay still so that my blood pressure and heartbeat registered low. My actions were not maniacal, no screaming and thrashing, another good sign. And asking to speak with the authorities should be put on the plus side. As soon as Nurse Sarah was done, I planned tell her that I was hungry. Desire for food was always a sign of good mental and physical health. Sarah continued to check my vitals, feeling my head for fever and pressing my wrists and angles for swelling with her bony fingers. I stayed calm and it all had to look good.

It was not easy to keep my sincere face from curling up into anger. Although acting out now would feel good, but it would not do me any good. To be truthful with myself, I was slowly accepting the fact that I might have gone crazy yesterday, but I was not *that* crazy.

Knowing how much I needed this nurse's confidence, I asked, "How long will I have to stay in this room?"

Sarah checked her jeweled timepiece pinned to her collar. "You're on a twenty-four hour watch. Only a few hours to go."

"Then what happens?" I really needed to know.

"Depends upon your evaluation."

I nodded as if I understood. Then I said, "That sounds reasonable," as if I concurred.

She looked down and questioned me. "So you feel you should have been locked up?"

"In the light of day, and reviewing things through the eyes of others, I can see why being put here was thought to be the best alternative. But, I do not think I should be here ... now."

She pulled out her penlight and checked my eyes.

"When do I get the eval?" Using the shortened version, I tried to sound professional.

"Let's start with a glass of water and a bowl of soup, shall we?"

Making a happy face, I made sure to sound innocent, almost childlike. "I'd love that!"

Sarah turned, walked away without expression and locked the door behind her. I was left by myself, but was a I really alone? Scanning the room, I found pinpoint camera lenses peeking out at me from several places ... especially from each one of the four corners.

The door opened again and two CNAs, one male and one female, entered. I could figure out that the male was there strictly to stand guard over any temper tantrums while the female held a tray in her hand. When I tried to sit up in order to sip the water she was offering, he brought out two pillows from under the bed. He pushed them under my head giving me the ability to swallow. I could not wait for that straw to be put in my parched mouth.

I sucked the glass of water dry. She pulled out the straw and fed me spoonfuls of broth that tasted like salty bath water, but I took it down and licked my lips for more. After finishing the third course of lumpy green gelatin, I smiled. "I need to go to the bathroom?"

The male spoke up. "Who you trying to kid. You're catheterized."

I hated this power freak's arrogance and filed him away as a piece of dog crap, but kept a sweet smile on my face. "Oh, thank you. I didn't realize."

His misshapen face wore a smug smile as he bragged, "I should know, I did it myself."

I smiled back, thinking how he would be the first to get it if he foolishly untied my straps. But, that was my secret ... for now.

Trying again I asked nicely, "Do you know when they're going to do the evaluation?"

He ignored my question, but she spoke up. "Within the hour, so try to stay calm."

When they left and locked the door behind them, I worked cautiously to try and slip my hands free. Humming a little tune, I pretended to stretch in order to cover why my hands were moving. Try as I might, those damn straps would not give.

Frustrated and working up a sweat, I stopped when I saw the door open again and Kyle Marx walking into the room. The look on Kyle's face unnerved me.

He was not alone. Two distinguished looking men accompanied him. Behind them were two burly CNAs whose genders were not discernible. They began unlocking my straps and showed mercy by helping me sit up. I turned and let my numb feet dangle to the floor as my blood began circulating again up to my brain. I thanked them both as they left the room.

Looking at the three standing in front of me, it was the bald man who first introduced himself. "My name is Dr. Scanlan." He smiled. "I'm a psychiatrist." He pointed to the grey-haired man with deep blue eyes standing next to him. "This is Dr. Steele. He's a psychologist. We've been sent here by Dr. Saville. He's concerned about this situation and wants to understand what ultimately happened to bring you here."

My heart skipped a beat at the sound of Dr. Saville's name. Although I felt respect and admiration for him, I remembered that it was his written alert sent back to Barrington Hall that put me on the Watch List for possible depression that started this problem.

I smiled meekly at the two doctors standing in grey and navy suits. All the while, a warning to be careful crawled along the back of my mind.

Dr. Steele stepped closer and looked straight into my eyes. "Would you like the two of us to be listed here at Barrington Hall along with your doctor of record?"

Marx interjected, "That's not possible. We have our own staff."

"If at all possible, I want to work with these gentlemen."

Marx's forehead furrowed, showing that he did not like where this was going. "We have holding power until Ms. Hennessey is seen and released by both our psychiatrist and Dr. Saville. Add to that the twenty-four hour observation, she'll be here at least another day."

The soft spoken Dr. Scanlan shook his bald head. "I represent Dr. Saville and have his permission to act on Ms. Hennesy's behalf. Your psychiatrist will have to confer with me?"

The Assistant Director's face flushed. "Do you have that in writing?"

"I can have it faxed." He pulled out his cell, "You can talk to Dr. Saville while we wait?"

Kyle stepped towards the door. "Let's go to my office."

Neither doctor moved. Dr. Steele asked, "What about getting her out of here?"

Marx was now beet red. "Again, her behavior yesterday warranted this lock down."

I wanted to scream. Instead I asked, "What *will* it take to get me out of here?"

"I can't let you go before the twenty-four hours and you must have the evaluation."

I tried to be funny. "So many doctors with names beginning with the letter S?" When no one laughed I asked, "Could I finish my time in a room with a toilet and get my stuff back?"

Both men turned to face Kyle, waiting for his positive answer.

Dr. Steele added, "Surely, you have secure rooms available on this floor that would provide better accommodations?"

Kyle sighed, "I guess that could be arranged." He turned to stare down at me. "But I must warn you, Ms. Hennessey, if there's another show of hostility or more accusations...." He stopped to let the tiny muscles in his face twitch. "You'll be brought right back to this room."

"I understand." And I decided that there would be no silly talk coming out of my mouth about the tunnel, the crazy clown or that sneaky dog.

Chapter Thirty

Kyle turned to the two doctors and began his corporate babble. Once again, he tried to sell Barrington Hall's security decision to lock me up. "Naturally, it was for Ms. Hennessey's own good and the welfare of the other patients." All the while, he kept backing up to the door. I could see that he wanted to steer the doctors away from me, physically and psychologically.

Dr. Scanlan turned his back and engaged Kyle in specifics. Kyle answered some, but backed away from the others by stating, "We'd have to bring the Director into that conversation." The psychiatrist kept probing, but Marx kept maneuvering around the hard questions.

Dr. Steele did not join their conversation. Instead, he kept staring at me. At first, I wondered if he was making a psychological decision until he surprised me. Without moving a facial muscle, his right eyelid dropped down and blinked. It was not an overt wink that any of the cameras could pick up ... still?

For no reason that I could understand, I made an urgent request. "Could the doctors stay with me for a few minutes."

Kyle stopped and Dr. Scanlan stepped back with a smile. "Of course, we promised Dr. Saville we'd visit and check on your knee." He looked back at Marx, "You don't mind?"

Kyle looked ready to protest and moved in between the two men, but Dr. Scanlan patted him on the shoulder. "You can rest assure we'll take good care of her."

"I'll expect that you will both stop in my office on your way out?" Kyle looked angry.

Dr. Steele spoke up. "Count on it. There's more we want you to tell us."

Marx left and they smiled, waiting for me to speak. "Thank you for coming and helping me. Can you explain what their evaluation will involve?"

The handsome Dr. Steele thumbed back to Dr. Scanlan. "He'll give you a better answer."

The psychiatrist explained that the questions did not have right or wrong answers, only right or wrong attitudes. As he spoke to reassure me, I watched Steele out of the corner of my eye and came to the realization that he was not a medical man, nor a doctor of psychology.

Steele picked up on my revelation and knew that his game with me was up. He smiled sheepishly and glanced down at the floor. I could not leave it alone, and while the good doctor Scanlan expressed his confidence in my ability to get through the simple evaluation, I winked back at the tan, very handsome, man who I seemed to recognize from past meetings.

A vision of how I appeared made me suddenly feel self conscious. My hair, stinking and matted, hung in my eyes. My face, scabbed and blotchy from the ant bites. The wrinkled hospital gown, barely covering my backside and certainly not hiding my connection to a urine bag.

Dr. Scanlan stopped talking about the eval and both stood looking at me. Curiosity overrode my embarrassment and I touched Steele's well manicured hand. "Who are you?"

The real doctor turned to the imposter and said, "Catch up with me downstairs."

Steele's blue eyes scanned the room before he said, "Today, I'm a doctor. Yesterday, I searched for you looking like Elvis." He stopped to chuckle."You should've seen me swivel my hips." He winked, "You once saw me in a Roman collar."

I was careful to pretend to cough, when I asked, "You're one of Luc Raines boys?"

He brought out a white handkerchief and pretended to sneeze. "One of his boys? I'd say more like a sidekick." We laughed and it felt good.   He let the moment linger, then whispered through the linen. "What's going on here?"

I used my hand to cover my mouth. "The mental patient? Did they capture him?"

He smiled and said out loud, "Yes! There's a storm coming."

"Darlene's the patient who says her boyfriend, Harold, murdered Genevieve."

"Yes! I played the game of CLUE as a kid." He laughed over his made-up line.

Coughing again for cover I said, "What's interesting is the dog showing up here."

His sky blue eyes narrowed and I felt he was debating with himself whether to tell me a secret. Instead, he sneezed again into his handkerchief and asked, "What dog?"

"Pat'll tell you about our Georgetown case."

"Who hired you?'

"Unknown!"

Questioning me with his eyes, he made me feel awkward. The explanation was too long to repeat. Besides, Pat had passed this intel on to Luc Raines. How much of it was dispersed to Luc's men was not my business. Perhaps he asked duplicate questions of me to verify Pat's story?

He bent down until we were close enough to kiss. "What was in the note?"

"Pick through the trash. Call if anything was unusual."

"And did you?"

"Pat sifted it, but found nothing."

"What about that phone number?"

"It was off the grid." I waited for him to offer an explanation. I already knew that being off the grid makes the number covert and not necessarily a government number. Hackers were expert at setting up a bogus number and routing calls around the globe.

"Did Pat call the number?"

"I don't remember." I lied. "You'll have to ask Pat." I wanted to be open with this very handsome, very pleasant man ... but, I was not ready to trust him.

"Okay." He kept looking into my eyes as he sat on the bed. "Tell me about the Bazaar."

"You mean the bizarre happenings at the Bazaar?"

He chuckled. "That bizarre day you experienced was only yesterday."

My head spun trying to comprehend all that had taken place in one day.

"Do you feel up to talking about yesterday?"

"Yes. It was yesterday that I spotted that same dog running along the First Floor."

He whispered in my ear. "You're sure it was the same dog?"

I worried about my breath, but whispered back, "So sure, I followed him into the woods."

He smiled and asked again, "Why'd you think it was the same dog?"

Not wanting to divulge the dog's name, I worked around it. "Running in the rain, holding bags of garbage with a canine nipping at my ankle. Don't you think I'd remember it?"

He burst into laughter and I joined him.

Chapter Thirty-One

Steele left, promising to get doctor privileges and twenty-four-hour access to the facility while I remained there. I thanked him, but knew that his request would be difficult to obtain.

He had not been gone a minute when Nurse Sarah returned. Still no smile, but I smiled at her when she announced that her visit was to remove the catheter. She must have had a lot of practice because it was out in a millisecond. I was happy to see her go and leave the door ajar. I got up and walked around the room to relax my cramped leg muscles.

Lyrie was the next to bounce through the open door. Her news was good. My things would be brought up as I was being transferred to another room while staying on the Third Floor. Trying to weasel information, I asked a leading question. "Did you spot that dog last night?"

"What dog? You keep talking about a dog?" Her face wrinkled up in frustration.

I sat down on the bed and changed the subject. "Damn fire ant bites are distracting me."

"That's another thing. There are no fire ants in Virginia."

My level of frustration kept escalating. There were so many people denying the existence of that dog and now those ants. I tried to explain again. "Talk to Tomas. It was all his fault. He said the pets were locked up in the Shower Room and that this one dog kept getting away."

"Tomas works on-call and he won't be back till the holidays?"

"He had the dogs corralled in the Shower Room. One escaped!" I tried again.

"So, you're talking about one of the pets brought here to visit with the patients?"

"No." I shook my head. "Wait! Now, I'm confused. Forget I even said anything."

Lyrie tried to joke with me. "You really like dogs. It's all you talk about ... dogs."

"Let's not talk about it." I waved off the subject. "When can I take a shower?"

She leaned close. "Forget the shower. You're in lockup. Think of yourself as lucky to be leaving this padded room. Just go along with what they offer and stay straight till morning. No funny stuff, or you'll never get released. You do want to go see your doc and get released?"

"Yes, I want to get out of here." I made a happy face. "Did they order my medivan?"

It'll be here at ten. You must behave till then." The strange way Lyrie looked at me made me wonder if she thought I might not make it through the night, might not be ready to go see Dr. Saville in the morning. Maybe, she thought I was mentally incapable after all?

I grabbed her arm. "Please, Lyrie, I'm not crazy. You have to believe that?" She patted my hand, trying to release my grip. "Lyrie, I've been through a lot and my nerves are shot!"

Lyrie's soft manner returned. She put her arm around me and whispered. "Calm down. I'm acting strange for another reason ... something I'm not supposed to discuss."

"No secrets. Tell me, what's going on?"

Her eyes rolled up. "A hurricane's coming up the coast, heading for the Chesapeake Bay."

"Mother of Mercy! Now, I really do want to get out of here."

"You're better off here if the worst happens." When her cell rang, she waved good-bye.

Nurse Sarah passed Lyrie in the doorway. Surprisingly, she came in wearing a smile. "I'll take you to your new room."

I was quick to follow and moved fast alongside her. Putting one foot in front of the other did not seem to be an effort. Still, I felt dizzy and my ears kept closing. I told this to Sarah.

"It's the barometric pressure. There's a storm coming."

I appreciated her candor. Not wanting to seem manic, I did not ask for more information.

Walking along the hall I noticed changes. While the area we had just left had prison decor, this part of the floor had wooden doors with shades on the inside of the windows.

My eyes kept searching to see who lived inside each open door, but the rooms were mostly inhabited. The others were mostly empty. I turned to Nurse Sarah. "Where's everyone?"

She kept walking. "They like to congregate in the Day Room and enjoy the morning."

"Where's that?" I heard a television blasting somewhere up ahead accompanied by low murmuring. As we approached the double-glass doors on the right that stood open, I saw a group of fully dressed people. Young and old, they stood around a big screen, focusing on a weather report. Looking closer, I recognized the grimace of anxiety and fright wrinkling their faces.

As we walked past the Day Room, each head turned to look at me in a strange way. Their odd stares seemed to size me up and question my ability to attack and hurt them. I suddenly felt like a wild animal being brought to new cage at the zoo.

Glancing back at the weatherman pointing to the white swirl positioned on the Mid Atlantic coast, I caught the red crawl moving across the bottom of the screen. It read:
STORM WARNING SEVERE WINDS-LANDFALL EDGING TOWARDS THE BAY.

The news that a storm might impede my leaving Barrington Hall brought all my anxiety back and my skin began to itch. Looking up, I saw that Nurse Sarah had walked ahead of me and was waiting at the last door on the left. Seeing the emergency door to the stairwell at the end of the hall made me feel better.

When I caught up to Nurse Sarah, we both looked through the door's window. The room was tidy and contained a bed, dresser. toilet and sink. She quipped, "All the comforts of home."

When she unlocked the door, I practically fell into the bed. "I feel so tired."

She pulled up the covers and for the first time her face softened. "You need a few hours of rest. Chemical sleep is not restorative. You need natural sleep." She walked over to the small window, too tiny for a body to climb through, and pulled down the shade. The room darkened against the cloudy sky. As she walked away, I followed her instruction and fell into a deep sleep.

Chapter Thirty-Two

I felt a tug on my arm and woke up to see Lyrie and Mary smiling down. It took me a second to realize that I was not down in room 112. And had to ask, "Did they give away my old room?"

Mary laughed the loudest. "Are you kidding? This place is worse than a hot sheet joint. Empty beds don't last long here. Two accident victims came in last night. Best drinking buddies out celebrating and can't remember who was behind the wheel."

Lyrie added, "Cheryl wakes theses fellas full of broken bones every morning. Screaming at them to get up and push themselves to the gym for physical therapy. Can you imagine?"

I nodded. "Poor bastards!" The phrase fell off my tongue. "I'm not poking fun at them. Just remembering Cheryl, my favorite task master!" All three of us laughed.

Looking past the girls, I saw the cart loaded with my belongings. It made me feel human again to see my clothes and especially my shoes to cover my bare feet. I was anxious to wash and get dressed, but stopped cold seeing the black duffel bag that Pat had brought to me. I suddenly missed my partner and friend.

"Have we heard how Pat is doing?"

"She had her surgery. It went fine and she'll be released soon." Mary answered.

"She can walk?" I asked.

Lyrie laughed. "Not yet. She'll be on crutches for a few weeks."

Wanting to call Pat, I realized that both cell phones were in my pants pockets when they came after me. I asked, "Do either of you have my cell phones?" Both girls looked sheepish.

Mary said, "No phones are allowed on this floor. They probably have them at the Nurse's Station. When they take you down in the morning to catch the medivan, be sure you get them."

"I can't have them now?" I tried to keep my voice matter-of-fact.

Lyrie shook her head. "Sorry, no outside communication up here."

"That sounds reasonable." I said, not wanting to sound belligerent. "I need to wash up."

"We can't help you." Mary smiled too sweetly. "I'll send in your CNA."

As soon as she closed the door, Lyrie handed me my necklace with the key to Base A. "I slipped this off you before they took you inside last night."

I let her put it in my hand, but offered no explanations. She hugged me and left.

Casually, I searched through my things. While I pulled out clothes to wear, I saw that my nail file was also among the missing. I vowed not to be angry and only concentrate on my homecoming tomorrow. And a few days after that, Pat and I would be laughing over a glass of wine about this entire adventure.

A male CNA entered with towels and wash cloths. He left without saying a word and I got busy at the sink removing the grit and perspiration. After I wiped dry with the towel, it showed a thick white cream that must have been applied to my face while I was knocked out. Without a mirror, it was difficult to see if I had removed it all. I was glad that the swelling in my cheeks was mostly gone. Even the tiny ant-bite scabs were beginning to fall away.

Feeling fresh and dressed in clean clothes, I felt hungry for real food. The same male CNA brought in a tray with my favorite dinner of meat loaf, mashed potatoes and green beans. The only difference was that up here the food was presented on paper plates with a plastic spoon. It did not matter. I was ravenous and began devouring the food by the time he reached the door.

As I sipped the black coffee from a paper cup, Nurse Sarah came in and asked, "Ms. Hennessey, are you ready to take your evaluation?"

"Yes. Who's going to administer it to me?"

"Follow me. We'll go to the consulting room."

I let her lead me into the hall, past the Day Room on the left where my fellow inmates were still gathering around the big screen still reporting the storm. They paid no attention as I walked by and I guessed that they now considered me one of their own.

Entering a bare office, Nurse Sarah sat behind a small desk. She bid me to take the only other chair opposite her and I obeyed. There was a clipboard waiting with several papers. I tried to glance at it, but she pulled it close and began to scan what looked like a questionnaire.

"Are you going to give me this test?"

"It's not a test. It's an evaluation. I will administer it, if that is all right with you?"

"Of course, I have no objection."

"Your responses will only be yes or no. Tell the truth. There are no right or wrong answers. This is intended to give us a snapshot of your thinking."

My heart began to pound, pushing my blood pressure higher. I worried about telling the truth. I worried about how I would react to some of their questions. Folding my hands in my lap, I waited while she shuffled papers in and out of the clipboard.

"Number one, are you willingly answering these questions?"

I suddenly felt as if I was on trial. "Yes."

"Number two, do you consider yourself sane?"

I took a deep breath. "Yes."

"Number three, do you ever talk to animals?

Silver's face came to mind along with my kindergarten's pet turtle, Roscoe. "Yes."

I watched Sarah's lips move as she pre read each question before she asked it out loud. After I gave her my answer she made notations. Taking it alone would have been preferable.

"Number four, do you ever talk to plants?"

I smiled and gave an emphatic, "No!"

In the back of my mind, I wondered how these simplistic questions were slanted? Should my answers be all yes, or all no? Or, was each question and answer judged on its own merit?"

"Number five, do people tend to stare at you?"

Although she was staring at me right then, I answered, "No."

"Number six, do people laugh at you behind your back?"

This one was not going to be easy. How would I know whether people were laughing at me behind my back? They could be laughing at me, especially here. Still, how would I know which meant that a yes answer could be construed as delusional. I blurted out, "No."

"Number seven, "Are you obsessed with death?"

I thought of all my departed loved ones. "No. No, I'm not."

"Do you know the question number that comes next?"

I played back my recent audio tape in my mind. Hoping to be correct I blurted out, "Eight." Something odd hit me. "That answer did not require a yes or no answer?"

She ignored my question. "Number nine, are you subject to fits of depression?"

Of course, I thought about being sad and depressed of late. It was the word, fits, that bothered me. My depression made me want to be alone. It did not cause me to have fits. "No."

"Number ten, are you plagued by strange coincidences?"

This questions was scary and could take me over the top. Hearing the question again in my head, I pinged on the word ... plagued. Although I had my share of coincidences, I never felt plagued by them. I was able to answer honestly. "No."

"Number ten, have you ever found an ant's nest and enjoyed stomping on all the ants?" Her eyes never left mine. I held her stare and did not blink.

"No." I told the truth. I did not find an ant nest. That militia of red ants found me.

Nurse Sarah tipped her head and tried to eye me into changing my answer. She waited for me to retreat from my original response. I did not back away.

Trying to keep my focus, I listened to every word as the questions kept coming. They went from silly and repetitious to stupid and downright frightening. I was generally able to answer with a negative response, holding my laughter on most. There was one question that Nurse Sarah asked that made me suck in my breath.

"Have you ever suspected that you might have gone insane?"

Rationalizing that the insane never accept their insanity. And the sane worry about going insane. My answer was, "NO!"

All through the drill, she never changed her expression. Neither did I.

"This will be the last question. Do you enjoy playing with firearms?"

I let this question run through my mind. Yes, I liked going to the gun range. I liked to shoot targets and felt comfortable when I wore a handgun on my person. But, I had a healthy respect for all weaponry. The word, playing, did not fit. I answered, "No."

Making her last notation, she moved to get up, but I needed an answer. "Did I pass?"

"What do *you* think?"

"I think the test wanted all NO ANSWERS!"

She smiled wide for the first time, "You interpreted the questions to be slanted to the negative, and yet? You took a chance and gave some positive responses?"

"Yes, because I wanted to answer honestly."

Chapter Thirty-Three

Although Nurse Sarah did not give me a score on the evaluation, her last comment made me feel confident. If they were going for honesty and principle, I passed. As she led me down the hall, the woman did not give me the impression that she worried about an insane female walking beside her. After letting me inside my room with her door key, she left without further explanation. I resolved not to let their evaluation bother me.

The room looked darker than when I had left it. Evening sky was coming on fast, but it was more than the setting sun making my ears buzz. Loud tinnitus, no doubt from the approaching storm, screamed inside my head. Laying back on the pillow, I tried to relax until I realized that I was hungry again.

No sooner had the thought crossed my mind, when my male CNA unlocked the door. I checked his name tag when he walked in the room with my tray. "Hi Bruce, glad to see you brought dinner."

When he set it down on my bed table, I spotted chicken soup and tiny ham sandwiches next to a brownie. Delighted, I grabbed the spoon.

"Sorry, there isn't more variety tonight. The storm's rolling closer and we're trying to get everyone fed so the kitchen staff can go home and be safe."

I swallowed a spoonful of soup and looked up at him. "How big a storm is it?"

He waved off my worry."You know the weather people. They love it when their airtime gets expanded and they can use phrases like 'packing winds' and 'blinding rain.'"

I laughed with him. Still, there was a nagging in my gut. "Could we be in danger?"

Bruce sighed and looked as if he was going to give it to me straight. "You're on the top floor under a heavy roof. This building made it through the last hurricane in 2003."

"I almost forgot about Isabel. We so seldom get hurricanes in the Washington area."

"That storm was a surprise. And remember how long the lights were out in Virginia?"

Nodding, I asked, "Is there an evacuation plan if the storm gets bad?

He smiled reassuringly, "Eat your dinner. Don't worry." He locked the door behind him.

It was that locked door that became unsettling. As I finished drinking the last of coffee, my mind kept wrapping around that door that I knew was locked. The more I thought about the locked door, the more I stared at the door handle that would not open the door. Anxiety kept building as I tried to come up with an exit plan that did not entail opening that locked door.

Frustrated, I concentrated on seeing Dr. Saville. In the morning I would be climbing aboard the ten o'clock medivan to drive me there and we would laugh. I continued to have happy thoughts until the buzzing, beeping and ringing in my ears got even louder. The pain became excruciating against the quiet in the room. It was too quiet. Why? Because there was no television. How could I go to sleep without a late night comic to entertain me?

I began pacing the floor, anything to make some sort of noise rather than listen to the fireworks going off in my head. Besides, I needed the exercise. My knee was feeling tight and everyone had warned me that inactivity would allow it to freeze-up.

Walking in circles now, I felt eyes watching me. No, it was not the pinpoint lenses making my hair rise on the back of my neck. Turning around, I spotted Nurse Sarah peeking in the door window and wondered how long she had been there.

As I walked up to the door, she disappeared. Looking out the window, I could not see any hall traffic at this end. Pressing my ear to the glass, I tried to listen above the cacophony in my head, but heard nothing. I wished that Nurse Sarah would come back and visit with me.

The room was getting darker and the ceiling light did not do much to brighten it. I ran to the window, stood on tiptoes and looked out. The grey twilight made it hard to distinguish the trees and bushes that seemed to wait like sentries for the storm.

I put my ear to the glass in the window and could barely hear the river rushing beyond the cliffs. I asked myself why I was becoming so antsy with only a few more hours left before dark. After my long stay here, the remaining time should be a snap and tomorrow it would be over.

The door swung open and Nurse Sarah came in with the little white cup containing my nightly meds. "Good to see you." I sat down on the bed and tried to make conversation. "What have you got for me?" I put out my hand and acted nonchalant. I knew the drill.

Sarah never spoke a word when she poured four pills into my open palm. I immediately recognized the pink one as my antihistamine that might help open my ears. The purple pill would keep my stomach acid from coming up my throat. The big white calcium pill would help mend my broken bones. And then there was the tiny yellow pill that I had never seen before.

When she presented the paper cup of water, I was glad to have it. Tossing all four into my mouth, I smiled at her while my tongue worked feverishly to find that tiny yellow pill. I leaned my head back, ready to swallow, when my tongue pushed that little stinker to the outside of my teeth. It stayed there while I took down the other three. To show Sarah that all four were sailing along their merry way, I stuck out my tongue and made a silly face. She looked satisfied and began to walk to the door.

"Nurse Sarah, I forgot ... what was that yellow pill for again?"

"It'll help you sleep through the storm tonight." She closed the door and I heard the key.

Marching to the box of tissues, I pulled out two and sneezed the yellow pill into them. Two steps away, I tossed the tissues with the yellow pill into the toilet and flushed. Wiping my hands I said out loud, "This is no night for you to be sleepy, Ms. Hennessey!"

Chapter Thirty-Four

Now, I had to play the part of a very tired patient. I got under the light blanket and turned on my side to stay focused on the door. The faraway sounds of the wind were getting louder and closer.

My eyes were glued on the glass inside the door as if it was a television screen. Wanting to see if anything or anybody moved in the corridor, I kept watch out there until the hall lighting dimmed. When the room darkened, my eyelids fluttered and drooped. Sleep came to take me away and I let it. Dreamland opened up, playing old black and white moving pictures on the back of my eyelids. Faded memories entertained me with old scenes from my childhood.

I stayed in that translucent place until my sensory alarm went off. Someone was putting a key in my door. Like a zombie, my body sat up. Still blind and not fully awake, I heard the now familiar voice of Bruce. "Ms. Hennessey?"

"Yes, what time is it?"

"It's only nine. Sorry to wake you."

Before I could finish saying, "What's going on?" My feet were on the floor.

"The storm is headed our way. I'm afraid we're going to have to tough it out."

I opened my eyes, trying to read his expression. "How bad is it going to be?"

"We have a couple of hours to prepare."

"Tell me the truth."

He never wavered. "The Capitol, Northern Virginia and Southern Maryland are all shut down. We're ordered off the streets asked to remain inside until it blows over."

"Thank you for leveling with me."

"The facility is short staffed. Some of the day shift left to tend to their families. Guys and gals like me, young and single, volunteered to stay." The eleven o'clock shift was canceled."

My shoulders drooped. "How many staff members will there be on this floor?"

"It's me and Sarah. That's all we got up here." Now his shoulders drooped.

"What about the first and second floors?"

"There's four workers for each floor handling residents that are high maintenance."

My head nodded to show my understanding. "Okay, I'll do whatever you say."

"I knew you'd understand."

"Do you have to keep me locked up? I could help out?"

"Up here? It's for your protection, believe me."

He did not have to say more. "I understand."

"I'm going to deliver food and water to everyone now. It'll get you through the night. Stay in your room and you'll be safe."

"What about the outside window?" I pointed to it.

"It's triple pane glass. Supposed to be bullet proof."

"What about the lights?"

"If the storm knocks out the electricity, there's a generator backup."

I still felt worried about that locked door. "Who's got keys to get in here?"

"Right now, only me and Sarah. It's an electronic door lock system that can be accessed remotely from security downstairs or with a key. If the power goes out and is not restored by the backup generator, the doors will automatically pop open per fire code."

"That gives me some comfort, but I wish I was still down on the first floor."

He chuckled, "I was just down there. It's a zoo. Frightened patients are wandering the halls, screaming and hollering. Trust me, it's much quieter up here."

"Why are they so upset downstairs?"

"High winds down in Richmond have knocked out all phone and cell service." He pulled out four bottles of water and some snack packages of cheese and crackers from the cart. "They feel cutoff from their loved ones. Being ground level, they worry about flooding."

"But, we're high on a cliff?"

"True. But, someone started talking about the nursing home flooding during Katrina.

I reached out for everything Bruce offered and stepped back as he closed and locked my door. Waving goodbye, I watching the young man turn his cart around and walk away. That little worrisome voice inside me wondered if I would ever get to see Bruce again?

Chapter Thirty-Five

The rolling sounds of thunder were no longer far away. They were creeping closer and streaks of lightning were coming along for the ride. Howling winds were sure to follow and I watched it all from the little window. I had to have been standing there for what seemed like an hour when I heard swishing sounds coming from inside the room. Turning around, I found the water swirling up to the rim of the toilet and wondered why? Could the pipes be shaking inside the walls? Or, was the building swaying in the wind?

My ears were closing again and I feared my loss of balance would come on soon. Since I did not want to fall, the best place for me was to get in bed and stay beneath the covers. I tried to do that for a few minutes, but soon went back. I could not leave that window.

When the howling increased, I surmised that it was the wind whistling through the trees. Listening closely, I realized that the high-pitch screaming was not coming from outside the building. It was coming from outside my door.

Leaving the wall window to walk across the room felt as if I was walking along a deck on the high seas. The floor was pitching and rolling. I waved off my loss of balance to closed Eustachian tubes and tried not to think about it as I made my way to the door.

With the lighting lowered, it was hard to see out in the corridor. I leaned up against the glass and listened. The painful screeching of male and female voices felt like a needle being poked in my ears. Stepping back, I cupped my hands over them, trying to ward off the madness. Too late, my own voice rose up to join the patients screaming on the THIRD FLOOR!

Out of control, I ran around and then ran back to the door. Grabbing the handle, I twisted and turned, but the lock held. The wailing and whining grew even louder from outside the door. I could only imagine the insanity if the patients up here were set free. My desire to escape the room subsided as the truth of what Bruce had said hit me. I did feel safer behind a locked door.

Surely an hour had gone by since that young man had waved goodbye. I could not tell. Searching my internal clock for the time, I felt it to be near ten. Only twelve hours and I would be sitting in Dr. Saville's office, laughing about this. I pictured that tall, handsome man writing my release order. And me telling him that I would send it back to Barrington Hall in the medivan. And when his dark blue eyes opened wide for an explanation, I would tell him how my plan included a ride home in a taxi.

Tapping noises began to sound at the wall window. How loud could they be, if my buzzing ears could hear them? I began to sing old songs out loud to test my hearing. If my voice could not be heard, I might be able to fix my ears by holding my nose and blowing hard.

My favorite repertoire were tunes by Huey Lewis. As always, I felt a twinge of guilt for not introducing the entire group: Huey Lewis and The News. And once again, I admitted to myself that I would never get over my teen crush on that man.

Taking a deep breath I belted out, THE POWER OF LOVE. My ears hardly heard my voice screaming the words. All of my vocal resonated only inside my head. I stopped to try and pop my ears open, but no luck. Changing tunes to, HEART AND SOUL, I could hear a small portion of my vocal. And that is when the loud bang hit my window as loud as a car crash.

No longer able to ignore what was going on outside, I hobbled a few steps until my knee froze and did not want to work. Changing weather was now my enemy. Everyone had promised that it would play havoc with the metal ring still inside my kneecap. They were not kidding.

Looking out the window into the darkness was difficult. The light from behind caused reflectivity on the glass making it hard to look out. I cupped my hands around my eyes and leaned forward until my nose touched the window.

My bird's eye view of the patio below took my breath away. Security high beams, mounted on the roof and sides of the building, allowed me to view the damage. Bushes and trees were being stripped bare by the high winds Leaves and branches were flying over the cliff while the naked tree trunks and shrubbery rooted in the red clay stood their ground.

The wind suddenly stopped and I wondered if the storm was over. Or, were we inside one of its rings of dead calm that the forecasters always talked about?

My mind wandered and I wondered where the tiny animals and birds hid out during storms. My heart sank thinking of the cooing chicks that had delighted everyone out on the patio these past weeks. We all knew the giant bushes were where Starlings nested and we stayed away.

My knee began heating up with inflammation but, before I could start over to the bed a large branch slammed against the window. The wind was flying at high speed, predicting the next round of storms would be even stronger. I stayed glued to the glass watching variety of stuff sail by: planters, wicker chairs and tables looked as if they were self propelled. Next came logs and roof shingles. Every airborne item looked out of place. Watching the flying objects made me dizzy. The visual was surreal.

I began to understood how roof jumpers, feeling they could they could fly, leapt off high building to jump into the wind. That thought had crossed my mind.

To stay focused, I kept pulling away from the window to look back at the room in my real world. What I was witnessing outside could have pulled me into its fantasy. I needed to keep thinking straight. Still, my curiosity kept bringing me back to the window. I wanted to watch!

The storm was building even higher this time. I could tell by the amount of unimaginable articles accumulating in the air swirling outside my third-floor window. As the air traffic coursed even higher, I had to bend my neck to look up and see what was up and away. With my hands cupped to the window again, I could feel the winds butting up against the building. When the window glass rattled, I did think about taking cover, but I could not leave. I had to stay and watch the show.

My tinnitus no longer protected me from the inmates ungodly howling inside and the storm unearthly howling outside. The odd spectacle coursing across the window only added to my loss of time and place. Every spark in my brain kept firing as I gazed at this aeronautical folly. And again, I suspected my own insanity.

The winds had to be blowing a hundred miles an hour and rising. Now, the tall bushes and small trees were being pulled out of the ground to join the strange flying parade that never ceased to end. Worse, I began to suspect that small animals were caught inside the wreckage now collecting in clusters as it passed by the window. Squinting, I searched for familiar shapes, but it was not easy to see inside the darkness.

Spellbound, I watched in horror as the parade of rubbish began winding closer to the building. The things flying in the wind became discernible. I could not turn away. Fascinated, I watched as the pageant moved nearer. Now, I could make out bricks and patio stones and shingles ... lots and lots of shingles ... shingles of all colors and sizes. So many shingles that I grasped the truth. Whole houses were being torn apart and dismantled by the storm still coming.

The flow of earthbound things kept flying by, faster and closer. I tried to calculate whether the ruins could bring damage to this stone building. There was so much audio and visual stimulus going on around me that I could not think to make that calculation. Watching that wind-driven train roll across the sky with its odd assortment of inhabitants was all that mattered to me.

The energy pushing things-that-belonged-on-the-ground swerved closer until small bits sticking out of the accumulation began bouncing against the side of the building. Logs and broken pieces of chairs smashed into the window and often stayed there for seconds before the surge pushed it forward again. Spellbound, I was afraid to blink and miss something..

The assortment was so thick now that it reminded me of a beaver's damn. There were entanglements of broken pots and pans, intertwined with furniture, rubbing against bicycles. So many oddities flew inside these soaring clusters that I began to call them out by name. "Twigs ... cup ... doll arm ... doll head ... plate ... broken plate ... shoe ... man's shoe ... furry head ... cat ... CAT?"

A black cat with green eyes had all four paws up against the window, looking in at me. Clinging to the glass for his life, the garbage behind him piled up and he screamed. In the next second, he was gone, pulled back into the junk pile moving skyward.

The wind kept raging, but the booming thunder was on its way. Larger objects were now scraping along the window. "Skate board ... tire ... bucket ... stroller ... shovel ... arm ... ARM?"

Lightning struck close to the building and lit up the window. In that flash, I could see mangled body parts strewn amongst building materials flying in the air. It was as if houses and all their contents had been ripped from the face of the earth and jettisoned into the air.

Another bolt of lightning struck above the building and lit up the ungodly sights sailing across the sky. The next clap of thunder and strike of lightning took out the lights. The building went dark, inside and out. I stood frozen, staring into blackness and waiting for the backup generator to come on. The storm kept blowing outside, but inside ... all was eerily quiet.

Without air conditioning cooling the building on this humid summer night, the steamy heat would rise quickly. Where was that generator? Sweat poured off me and ran down my body. I felt disoriented, but waited without moving a muscle for what seemed like an eternity.

I was amazed when my ears picked up a metallic click behind me. Wondering what it could be, I realized that it was my door unlocking ... just as Bruce had promised it would if the back-up generator failed.

While my eyes tried to adjust to the many layers of darkness inside, the wind outside grew louder. More trash piled up against the window from the thick debris field, but I could no longer see any of its contents. And for that I felt grateful.

Seconds later, I heard the squeak of a door hinge and knew that mine was being pushed open. Two slow footsteps entered sending a shiver across my shoulders. Caught off guard, I hoped my hearing was playing tricks with me.

Two more footsteps across the floor forced me to turn around and stare back into the dark room. More footsteps edged even closer to me. There could only be the bed between us now. I held my breath and waited for the attack.

Loud arguments and the sounds of fist fighting erupted out in the hall. Holding my breath, I kept trying to listen for any movement inside my room. There was none. The room felt empty as if I was alone again while the chaos in the hall escalated. Reaching out for the bed, I felt my way around it and headed to where I perceived the door might be located. The shrill voices of the insane, screaming and yelling, grew even louder.

My trips through the tunnel taught me how to take baby steps in the dark with my hands out in front of me like Helen Keller. And as I made my way, I promised the Almighty a contribution for the blind if I survived the night. When my fingertips found the door, it was still standing open. I stood in the frame and tried to listen. The commotion had moved down the corridor to the Nurse's Station, but still there were other patients wandering on their own in the corridor. Where was Nurse Sarah and Bruce?

Stepping into the pitch black hallway, I stayed to the right trying to avoid the Day Room where I suspected the inmates were gathering out of habit. My gym shoes slid quietly as I kept putting one foot in front of the other in the mounting heat and humidity. When a shift of air swirled behind me, I sensed that someone was on my tail. Hearing bare feet slapping the tile behind me ... one ... two ... three steps ... I sped up! Too late, the hard knuckles of a large fist smacked the back of my head making me fall forward on my nose.

I saw stars.

Chapter Thirty-Six

Down and down hard, I stayed on the cool tile while dazzling fireworks shot off inside my head. My mind and body needed the small reprieve from the living nightmare playing out above me.

Rough hands, a big man's hands, grabbed at my torso. The same hands found my armpits and began pulling me across the floor. All the while, he babbled. None of his words made sense. Even in my delirium, I knew the man had to be an inmate. Waking up, I wondered how he could see in the dark and where he was taking me?

Flipping over on my back, I wormed my way out of his grasp and scrambled to my feet. I staggered away, but he did not follow. I wrote the attack off as a patient acting crazy in this boiling pressure cooker that would only get hotter without air conditioning. I began to envision all of the Third Floor patients, myself included, dragging our feet with our arms out in the dark. The film, NIGHT OF THE LIVING DEAD, came to mind.

I needed to refocus and reminded myself that the Nurse's Station would be the best place to find a flashlight, or at least a penlight. Moving along the corridor, I was working my way against the foot traffic and kept dodging other wandering souls, who kept mumbling and crying. The pitiful people moving past me were probably on their way to the Day Room.

The whereabouts of Nurse Sarah or Bruce bothered me. They should have been in the hall, holding a flashlight and trying to corral us? A lump of fear formed in my throat.

Since each floor was laid out the same, it was easy to figure out where I was located even in the dark. Since the nurses were stationed across from the elevators, my plan was to find the elevators in order to find help. At least, that was what I kept reminding myself.

Taking tiny steps and waving my hands, I kept going, but I noticed that it had gotten quieter in front of me. The chaotic noise was now resonating from behind. My sense was that there were no hall walkers in front of me, so I moved to the left. Soon, I would be able to round the corner and find the bank of elevators. Across from the elevators would be the Nurse's Station where I could get help, or at least a flashlight.

The heat in the building kept rising and my body kept perspiring. My knee was screaming with pain forcing me to drag my right leg. There was no time to stop, but I added a handful of aspirin to my shopping needs. Feeling like an addict, I could hardly wait to get to the drug cabinet and planned to break the glass if I could not find the key.

The sound of hushed conversation up ahead made me stop. Trying to discern the words competing with the wind wailing outside and the inmates howling inside was impossible. Picking up a few phrases from the male voices, I realized that they were looters scavenging for drugs. What I questioned was the reason they were working in the dark and what had they done to Bruce and Nurse Sarah?

"Hey, what was that?" A deep voice ordered, "Jake, you better go check." Fast footsteps were coming because Jake was sent to find me. But, why was there no flashlight in Jake's hand?

My pounding heart warned me to turn and run. But if my floor map was correct, the laundry room was only a few steps ahead. Sliding softly across the floor, I found the double-door entrance to the utility room and ducked inside. I closed the doors behind me and took a big breath of relief. An ungodly stench of soiled linen, hot and steamy, hit me in the face and I wanted to cough. Holding my nose, I felt around and found a pile of sheets. I dived inside them and gagged. Seconds later, the doors opened. Still, no flashlight shined in my eyes?

Jake hollered out, "HOLY SHIT! Who the hell died in here?" The doors slammed shut.

Supposing that Jake would report back to his cohort that he did not find any interlopers, I waited. Ready to face the looters rather than breathe the stagnant air any longer, I found the double doors. Returning to the hallway, I looked for any lights.

Although it was still dark, the gruff voices were gone. All that could be heard were the sounds of fighting and screaming back by the Day Room. I could only imagine their torment.

Waiting for the courage to continue to the Nurse's Station, I stood in the doorway. Time seemed important to me all of a sudden as if I had been tasked to keep track of it. The clock in my head had not registered hours, minutes or seconds since the first signs of the storm.

As I realized that my urgent need to resolve my lost time calculations might have been my brain trying to keep me out of harm, a male voice shouted to someone down by the Day Room. "Don't go to the Nurse's Station. There's bad men down there. They'll hit you!"

An elderly female voice responded, "I need my meds or I'm going to start biting soon!"

I reasoned that the crowd back there had already tried to reach the medicine cabinet and had run into the looters. Needing their medications, they would soon make another run for it.

Finally, my feet took me into the corridor where the air was clean smelling. Turning left, I kept my left hand on the wall and kept going until the wall ended. Turning left, I felt the elevator doors and turned around to cross over to the Nurse's Station.

Feeling my way to get to the raised desk, I almost tripped. I had forgotten about the two steps that rose on both sides. When I bent down to search with my hands, I found something else ... a body, a man's body, a man's DEAD BODY!

I flew back and stifled a scream. Bending down again, I tried to shake the man by his shoulders to make sure, but there was no response and his hand felt lifeless. Ashamed of myself, I searched his clothing in the dark. I could feel that he had on cotton scrubs like any medical staff member. His pant pockets were empty, but when I reached up to the pocket on his chest there was a pen shape. Pulling it out, I found the clicker.

The tiny circle of light made me smile, but seeing Bruce, dead at my feet, made me weep. His eyes were open, staring up with a look of wonder. The young man must have been surprised from behind by the knife sticking out of his neck.

When I used the tiny light to search around the desk, I saw the medicine cabinet's broken doors hanging off their hinges. Cringing, I surmised that Nurse Sarah had not given up the keys. My aching knee reminded me to check for aspirin. Pulling open the drawers below, I found a bottle and pushed it inside my bra.

Loud screaming made me search the hallway. The penlight picked up the demented faces of angry people. Flashing the tiny beam across their eyes, made them stop pushing and shoving to hold up their arms against the sudden light. When I turned off the penlight. I could hear their bare feet falling and tripping over each other.

I needed to get away. I needed to get off this floor.

Of the two stairwells, one was next to my room and the other was located to the right of the elevators. Both were kept locked to keep foot traffic under the watchful eyes of personnel and cameras. The stairwell doors should have also unlocked when the generator failed.

Stepping over Bruce's body, I made my way to the stairwell across from me. The metal door felt cold to my hands as I pulled on the handle. I prayed that the insane patients did not hear me as I slipped inside the stairwell.

Chapter Thirty-Seven

Closing the heavy door, I stood with my back against it and waited. Looking around, it was even darker inside the stairwell. Listening, I was surprised to hear the wind whistling around the building. I wondered how I could have forgotten about the storm?

The door knob rattled behind me. Bracing my body, I tried to hold back the door with all my energy. Mounting pressure kept getting stronger until it blew open the door and slammed me up against the wall behind it. The heavy metal door pressed me against the bricks while the angry mob beat on each other and fought to get into the stairwell.

Sandwiched between the wall and the open door, I let out a scream. No one heard me. How could they? They were howling like a pack of wolves. Fighting each other: punching, kicking and biting like animals. Still they kept coming, stampeding through the doorway.

I heard their frightened cries of anguish as they lost their footing in the dark. In their haste to reach the stairs, they began tripping and falling and piling up at the top of the metal staircase. The crowd kept pushing while the weak fumbled to find the stairs. The crowd kept shoving while more stumbled over each other until they tumbled down. Piled up below, they cried out in pain paralyzed with broken necks and back bones.

I wanted to scream out; I wanted to warn them. They were going to kill each other if they did not stop fighting. But, how could any of them even hear me above their own screaming and yelling?

The clamor of their final massacre was so offensive to my ears that my hands flew up to shut it out. Still, they kept pushing. I was grateful to stand in the dark and not see the carnage.

Then it all stopped. The frenzied activity faded leaving an emptiness in the stairwell. My hands dropped from my ears and I listened, but there were no sounds. I sensed that the patients acting like savages were no longer alive because I could no longer feel their energy around me.

Still pushed flat against the wall, I could hardly catch my breath. The rancid air smelled sickeningly sweet, reminding me of the old butcher shops that put saw dust on the floors. While I stood there taking tiny breaths, the heavy door fell away from me and closed on its own.

Once again, the storm became audible. Only this time, I could feel its energy grinding like a freight train. Frightened that the roof was going to blow, a new urgency came over me. In order to survive, I needed to get into the basement. Before I could take a step, guilt made me call out, "Storm's Coming!" No response. "Hey folks? We gotta go to the basement!" Silence.

I did not turn on the penlight when I opened the door and walked out of the stairwell. I did not want to take those gruesome visuals to appear in my nightmares. Stepping inside, I moved the penlight's tiny spot around the corner from the Nurse's Station. There was Sarah's half-dressed body sprawled on the floor. Her face was mangled and bloody. If I had not seen her name pin, I would not have recognized the woman. Her hand felt lifeless. Mesmerized by the manner of her violent death, I could only wonder if she had been beaten to death by the looters or her own patients?

I walked back to my room feeling sad. Being able to see with the penlight made it so much easier to navigate. The floor was quiet now and looking around at my things, I realized that the two water bottles were the only things of importance. I chugged one right there with three aspirins and brought the other with me.

Leaving my room, I opened the emergency door next to it. The staircase looked empty and I started my descent. Ignoring the intense pain in my knee, I took two and three stairs at a time. When I got to the basement and opened that door, I was surprised not to see people hovering together down there for safety.

Running to the Security Office, I saw no signs of life. Where were the guards?

The roar of metal bending from above convinced me that the storm was pulling off the roof. Without it, the building's structure would be next. Needing to take cover, I surmised that the best place would be the old gym. Surprisingly, I found the door wide open and ran inside. The place looked the same. Piles of junk still stood taller than me and littered the floor. Still, I wondered where were the other people?

Rushing to get to the back wall, I felt tremors below my feet as if the building was breaking apart. Running through the old gym, I saw the cabinet pulled away from the wall. The tunnel door was open and waiting.

My head and my heart did not want to go inside ... again.

The trembling increased, shaking the tall piles of old exercise machines. The heavy metal began to slide and pull away from the piles to take flight. The flying machines zoomed in circles midair and across the floor. Piles were dropping to the floor. My only escape was the tunnel.

As I ran inside, the large cabinet crashed to the floor behind me.

With the penlight showing the way, the inside did not seem as scary.

Running the long tunnel, I wondered if I was the only one in the building left alive. And then, I wondered if I had a chance of staying alive. Crashing sounds from above made me think that the building's upper floor was being dismantled by the wind. I tried not to listen as I ran.

Stopping to catch my breath and wipe the salty perspiration out of my eyes, I was surprised to look down and see that I was still clutching the bottle of water in my left hand. Hot and thirsty, I unscrewed the top and drank it down. Still panting, I tried to slow my heartbeat now pounding inside my ears.

As my internal buzzing softened, I picked up the echo of not too distant voices. The muted conversation seemed to be originating from the laundry, which I thought was located left at the cross tunnel. Standing there, waiting for my breath to return, the smell of smoke wafted past my nose. Was the building on fire? No! This was stale smoke ... cigar smoke.

Excited to think there might be others who had taken refuge in the basement, I sped up. With the empty bottle in one hand and penlight in the other, I resumed my flight to look for safety. Approaching the intersection, I slowed down. Something made me question whether there was something or someone up ahead ... hiding in the dark ... waiting.

The small spot of light revealed nothing as I crept closer to the intersection. Before I could shine the light into the cross tunnel, a man's meaty hand reached out and grabbed my hair. My head jerked to the right and the penlight dropped from my hand as I tried to fight off the hand. When the penlight rolled forward ... away from us ... we were left struggling in the dark.

My head kept pulling away from his grip. Over and over, his giant hands kept grabbing more of my hair. He pulled tighter and handfuls of my thick hair ripped out at the root. The pain was excruciating. And yet, I kept scratching and pushing him off me.

When I lost my balance, we both fell down and my body landed on top. Still clutching the open bottle, I instinctively shoved the neck end into his face. Twisting, I hoped that the plastic edges would rip and that a jagged piece would burrow into his flesh.

He rolled my body back and forth until he gained momentum and fought his way to be on top. His strong hand got the bottle away from me and we fought savagely with our bare hands. He went for my throat and I went for his eyes. He choked me and I pushed my thumbs into his eye sockets. I held my breath until the pain in his eyes forced him to let go of my neck. When I tried to push him off, he used his legs to keep me down. Back at it, we were pulling hair and scratching faces. Now it was a cat fight and since my nails were longer, I won.

He scrambled to his feet and stood over me. "Don't think you're going to get away." Recognizing his words, I knew the angry voice of Kyle Marx. "I'll never let you out of here."

I could feel the heat of his hatred as I struggled to stand up in the dark.

Before I could not escape his reach, Kyle's massive hand grabbed me by the throat again. He pushed me to the main kitchen and I could not stop him. A few steps more and his kick pushed open the steel door. A final shove sent me across the floor.

Catching my breath, I heard the door slam and hoped I was alone. Silence until a tiny flare ignited in the dark. The bright flame moved to a candle and lit up the room. There stood the Assistant Director, his eyes like a wild animal. He lifted the candle and searched for me. Unable to get up and run, he found me in a heap.

"There you are, you bitch!"

"How'd you know it was me in the dark?"

"I could smell you." He moved closer. "Why did you come here, anyway?"

Pushing back on my bottom, I said nothing. When I hit a wall, I stopped and so did his advance. Holding the candle out in front of him and staring down bleary-eyed, he smiled.

I caught a glisten in his eyes and wondered if I could reason with him. "Kyle?"

"Haven't you done enough already. What do you want?"

Hearing his slurred speech I asked in a small voice, "What have I done to you?"

"You tried to fool me. But I caught you!" He leaned back and laughed like a hyena.

"That doesn't make sense. Why would I try and fool you?"

Swaying above me, I wondered if the building could be bending in the wind again.   "You're nothing but a little snoop and you've caused all my trouble here. Who sent you?"

"Kyle, my surgeon sent me here after reconstructing my knee. You know that."

His upper lip rose high above his long teeth. Shaking his head he screamed above the storm. "You're slick. I bet you got a D.C. bouncer to cap you just so you could slide in here."

"What trouble are you talking about?"

"Don't you know? I'm being blamed for everything."

"Who's blaming you?"

"Wilder, of course?" Kyle whimpered like a sad child. "He wants me out. He hates me."

"Did you have something to do with Genevieve's murder?"

"No, but I covered it up."

"She wasn't killed by an escapee from the third floor?"

"Who the hell knows?" His mouth curled up. "Better yet, who the hell cares?"

"Where is the Director?"

"Hell, if I know. He's gone and set me up for everything. That's all I know."

"Kyle, it's only a job. You can get another."

His features softened. "You don't get it. It's not just a job. Working here is my means to be near the man I love!"

Shocked, and my face must have showed it, I had no words.

"Surprise! Surprise!" Kyle snickered down at me. "I was lured here by love."

"Was it reciprocal?"

"No. But, Wilder knew how to tease a fella into thinking it could be one day."

A loud crack sounded overhead and took the two of us by surprise. Screaming, I held my ears against the high-pitch destruction.

At first, Kyle acted lost in his own paranoia until finally he held up the candle and searched the ceiling with the flickering flame.

Taking advantage of his distraction, I got to my feet. When Kyle turned and found me upright, he went crazy. "Get back down on the floor?"

I yelled back. "The building's going to collapse!"

His black eyes stayed on me as that crazed smile returned.

"We have to hide from the storm. Can't you hear how it's going to tear down the building." I looked around the massive kitchen in the dim candlelight and saw only counters and work tables. "Is there a stronger shelter down here?"

Kyle stood frozen, holding the candle and staring down at me, as if in a trance. His features began to twist into a ghoulish smile behind the shimmering flame until his head took on the shape of a sinister jack-o-lantern.

Watching his face contort, I came to the realization that Kyle had gone mad.

I took a deep breath and blew out the candle. Before he could lunge for me in the dark, I bent down and stayed low. Pain shot through my knee, but I kept creeping away.

Kyle kept calling out to me, using a variety of insulting words. When I found the open door, I stood up and took off. Running past the cross tunnel, light sprang up on the right where my penlight waited. I stopped to retrieve it, but fell again when the building shook.

Crashing sounds from the floor above, convinced me that the roof had caved. Worried that the floors below it would come tumbling down, I ran to the Laundry Room and banged on the metal door until it opened. The blinding light made me hide my eyes, but I could hear the friendly voices welcoming me.

There was one shouting above the rest. "Hey, Girlfriend!"

"Darlene? Is that YOU?"

"Yeah, it's me. Glad to see ya made it."

HIDING PLACES AT BARRINGTON HALL

Chapter Thirty-Eight

Looking around in the candlelight, I saw that everyone there was ambulatory. Even Darlene was on her feet with a cane. My quick head count went past thirty and I saw that we were all patients.

I hugged Darlene and asked, "There's no staff down here?"

"Nurse Angela led us here and went back to help on the floor."

I saw a watch on Darlene's arm. "What time is it?"

She glanced down and said, "Ten twenty-five, why?"

"You would not believe what I've just experienced in less than an hour."

"If it's scary, please don't tell me. I'm dying for a smoke."

"Me too." I laughed.

"You don't smoke?"

"I'm ready to smoke anything right now." We laughed together.

Looking around, I was amazed to see giant washing and drying machines and a line of set tubs. I wondered out loud. "Do you think there's still water in the pipes down here?"

Darlene smiled. "Let's find out." She walked over and turned a spigot.

When fresh water came out, I cupped my hands for a drink. Darlene did the same. When the others saw what we were doing, they formed a line.

One of the men hollered out, "The lines should be clean. But as soon as you smell or see anything, stop drinking."

I was fascinated with the extremely large laundry machines. Walking over to a dryer, I opened the door and saw the amount of room inside. I checked out the washer and found the same amount of room inside that drum.

Counting the machines and the number of people standing with us, I could see that there was enough room. Before I could explain this last ditch survival plan, the building felt as if it was being pulled out of the ground. Everyone around me held on to each other. Darlene's eyes were ready to pop out of her head. I grabbed her hand and lead her to the closest machine.

Pulling open the heavy door with glass in the center, I motioned for Darlene to get inside. She shook her head, but I grabbed her hand again and helped her. It was not easy, but when I pushed her from behind it worked. All eyes watched me assist Darlene into the massive machine until they followed our lead. Another lady grabbed my hand and crawled in beside Darlene. I climbed in behind her and hoped our storm shelters would stay earthbound.

We hid inside the metal drums as the building was blown down around us. The huge laundry machines kept us safe while the wind and rain pounded down on Barrington Hall.

The dead calm finally arrived and stopped all the destruction. The ride was over. We climbed out and opened the metal door to the tunnel with trepidation. Seeing that the tunnel looked safe, we gathered together and I led with the penlight to the parking lot exit. When we pulled back the bolt on the exterior door, sirens were already blaring.

Chapter Thirty-Nine

Surviving patients from Barrington Hall still needing care were transported to other rehabilitation centers. The physically able were allowed to go home. I was one of those lucky ones. A volunteer driver took me to my small house, dodging fallen debris all the way.

"How bad is it?" I had to ask her.

"The hurricane swept through the Chesapeake and didn't calm down. It hit land around Annapolis and practically drove itself up Route 50 to the District. The destruction along the way wasn't bad, but it stalled over the Potomac River. And they think it gained strength from that body of rushing water. The cliffs on both the Maryland and Virginia sides caught the worst of it."

"What about Old Town Alexandria?"

"It flooded and is in a state of emergency."

"Just like the last hurricane in 2003."

When we turned the corner, both of our heads were spinning to see my neighbors houses. Most had gaping holes in the roofs where tree limbs had fallen. I was excited to see that my home had been spared. Missing window screens and broken glass were nothing to worry about.

It was near noon when the driver walked me up the front steps. Not that I had any of my belongings to carry, but she held my arm. "The street's deserted. Will you feel safe here?"

"Nothing can stop me from going in to my own house and sleeping in my own bed."

She smiled. "After last night, I can't blame you."

Seeing the code box on my front door, she turned away while I punched in the correct numbers. When the door swung open, happy tears filled my eyes."

She walked in behind me. "I don't know," she shook her head, "this might not be a good idea. The water and electricity are still off. Maybe, I should take you to a women's shelter?"

I put my hand up to stop her worries. "I'll be fine. Got plenty of food and bottled water."

It felt good to walk through the colonial hall leading past the staircase to the kitchen. Looking around at the immaculate kitchen and uncluttered counter tops, I was pleasantly surprised. "My sweet friend must've come over and cleaned my house."

"Okay," she looked concerned, "remember, the electricity's been off for twelve hours."

"I'll be fine. Just want to get out of these clothes and go to bed."

She smiled and handed me a card. "Here's the closest Red Cross Office, if you need help." I check it for her name and placed it on the island. "The land lines are down and cell service is sporadic. You're pretty much on your own here."

"Thank you, Deborah. You've been wonderful!"

We hugged goodbye and she made a promise. "I'll look in on you in the morning."

As soon as I closed the door behind her, I took off my shoes and walked barefoot back to the refrigerator. I needed the taste of cold beer. When I opened the door and saw no cans or bottles waiting for me, I was surprised. Pat might have enjoyed a few while cleaning up, or my son could have slipped into town to host a party while I was gone? Neither explanation rang true, but I was tired and the truth did not matter to me.

I grabbed a can of cola that was still cold and hoped there might be some warm water left in the pipes. The thought of a bath in my own tub delighted me. Climbing the stairs, it felt good to be home and have my freedom.

The second floor looked neat and clean, but I kept walking until I reached down and turned the nozzles for a hot bath. I climbed into a lukewarm tub and closed my eyes. Slinking down into the water felt heavenly. My head fell back and I decided to snooze in the afternoon.

It was dark when I heard the little tune playing from far away. I hummed along with it for a few seconds before I recognized the old melody: WILL YOU MARRY ME BILL.

While I laid below the cool water, enjoying the song, it hit me that Bill's cell was ringing.

Opening my eyes, I jumped up and slid across the tiles to get to his top dresser drawer. My wet hands kept slipping off the drawer pulls until finally I got it opened. There was the flashing red light, announcing an incoming call on his phone. I brought it to my ear and yelled, "HELLO!"

"Wow, you sound excited." Pat's deep voice was like manna to my ears.

"How did you get through?"

"Cell service stayed up, but it comes and goes as the governments and emergency crews utilize them. How are you?"

"Fine, now that I'm home." I smiled. "How are you? Where are you?"

"They kept me another day due to the storm. Besides, I need practice on my crutches."

"Smart thinking to call Bill's cell."

"You've had it rough. Lyrie told me how you got thrown up on the Third Floor. I made a phone call to get you assistance. Did it arrive?"

"All six feet of it arrived in a very handsome package calling itself a doctor."

She chuckled. "There's so much more I want to ask?" The line began to crackle.

"We'll have to talk over a bottle of wine." I laughed. "How about I pick you up and bring you here to recuperate. My house is still standing."

"Would love that ... hope we can ... cook." Her voice kept coming and going.

I was so intent on trying to hear Pat that I did not sense movement. When I did sense that I was no longer alone, my heart stopped.

A man's arm reached from behind and wrapped around my neck. My bladder squeezed with fear and wanted to let go.

A deep voice whispered in my ear. "Get off the phone!"

I was able to squeak into the cell, "bring potato salad," before my words were choked off and the phone was taken away.

Looking up at the dresser mirror, my heart raced. Looking back at me from the mirror was Wilder Wolfe. His tan features were lost in the dark, but I recognized his sexy stare and watched his mouth widen into a Cheshire smile. His white teeth were so bright that they glowed in the dark. "Thank you for not screaming. I won't hurt you. Please if stay quiet and listen to me."

Although Wolfe relaxed his hold, I was wrong to think he was going to let me go. No. He cuffed my free wrist and secured both hands behind my back. He seemed quite adept at doing it.

"Is this the way you get women to listen to you?"

"Give me a second to light a candle." He turned back to the chest of drawers.

I stood in the dark trying to clear my mind, trying to figure out if this man was here to hurt me. Two flames from the tall candles on the dresser gave us light. When Wilder moved one to the opposite wall, the candlelight warmed the room and I realized again that I was naked.

"Let me put clothes on, please."

His eyes looked up and down and up again. "I rather like you this way."

Moving back to the bed, I sat on the side and crossed my legs. "What *do* you want?"

He smiled as he mused, "Different time, different place? I could want a lot from you."

"Why are you here?" Another thought made me ask, "And how'd you get in?"

"Feeling the need to disappear, I searched the patient records. You were the only one who left an empty house behind and would not be leaving Barrington Hall for awhile."

"How did you get past the door code?"

"Oh please!" He tried to act silly. "Check out the spy shop in the District. There's tech stuff there that the spooks have been using for years."

"Can I get dressed?"

He picked up a candle and walked closer. "You look beautiful just the way you are."

"Then free my hands, please."

"Can't you wait until I leave?" His voice almost sounded tender and he almost looked sad.

"Okay." I agreed but added, "Talk to me. Why did you feel a need to disappear?"

"Oh my sweet lady," he sighed. "That's a long, long story and I won't bore you with it."

I nodded. "What's going on with Kyle Marx?"

His eyes narrowed. "Why would you ask about him?"

"Because he chased me through the tunnel and acted half crazy during the storm."

Wolfe laughed, stopped and laughed again. "Half crazy? Hell, he's completely crazy."

"Why did you hire him? Did he have something on you?"

He stopped laughing. "I hired Kyle because his past was checkered and inaccurate. For that reason, I felt I could trust him to stay to himself and not be curious about me."

"Kyle told me that he loved you?"

Wilder sighed and actually looked sad. "And that's when the problems began."

"Unrequited love is painful."

"Yes, and in Kyle's case it became destructive. He was out of control."

"You don't think he murdered Genevieve?"

"No, the only one Kyle wanted to murder was me."

"Now, the police believe the killer was a man named Harold."

"That's what I've heard."

"But, there was a patient on the Third Floor who kept escaping to run around the rooms."

"The facility tried to keep that floor restricted, but the staff's only human."

I kept asking myself why I liked this man's answers. "Wilder?" I softened my voice, "May I call you Wilder?" He nodded. "Why are you hiding at Barrington Hall?"

"Although I acted in a professional manner there, my background is a bit spotty."

Soft strains of a melody stopped us to listen. *Will You Marry Me Bill* rang out from inside the front pocket of Wilder Wolfe's khaki pants. He gave me a cold stare. "Who could that be?"

"You made me hang up on my friend!"

"Hmm? We'll pretend you're still taking a bath."

"If you plan to stay here, we better answer."

When he did not make a move, I knew my time with him was limited. As the phone kept playing the ringtone, I pictured our surreal scene and wondered what could be my next move. The music ended and the house fell silent again, but he kept his eyes on me.

"Do you have a plan?" My voice sounded weak. "Can I help you with it?" The melody started up again and I tried to convince him that we had to answer it.

He pulled out the phone and held it to my ear, keeping close to eavesdrop.

Pat's voice whispered soft and low. "Potato salad's coming."

Before Wolfe could pick up on her words, the line went dead. Before he could question me, I gave him an answer. "Sounded like a wrong number."

Wolfe placed the phone on the chest of drawers and smiled at me. "It's time to go."

"Please don't go without freeing my hands." He stopped to think about it. "Please?"

He came to the bed and released the plastic tie. My arms felt heavy and numb. I kept trying to shake them awake, but needles-and-pins were pinching the insides. The pain emanating from my upper limbs kept my attention until I heard the familiar rattle of the front door opening.

Wolfe heard it too. After days of living in my house, he had to be attuned to its sounds.

When I looked up for his reaction, Wilder Wolfe was no longer in the room and I was still naked. Running to my dresser, I hardly had the strength to pull out a pair of sweats. Before I could get dressed, the short stub of a revolver peeked around the door frame and I froze.

Chapter Forty

I could not stop staring at the very handsome, very tan man standing in the doorway who last called himself Dr. Steele. Dressed in white shorts and a navy polo, he looked odd holding out a .38 snub nose revolver.

Seeing me without clothes, he kept looking into my eyes. "Where is he?"

"He just left."

"I'll be back."

He left and I heard him searching the first floor.

My hands still tingled as they pulled on the pants and shirt. I had just gotten dressed when Steele returned. The gun in his hand had been replaced with a flashlight. He smiled, no doubt happy to see me wearing clothes. His deep voice asked, "Wolfe's gone. Are you okay?"

The next few weeks were chaotic. Everyone affected by the storm suffered. Still, the destruction and weeks of power outage were nothing compared to the loss of life. The fatality list did not show names that I recognized. The missing persons list did have a few that caught my attention: Kyle Marx, Wilder Wolfe and Beck.

A month later, I tapped the horn in Pat's driveway and she exited her house looking gorgeous in a black lace dress. Her long hair flowed softly in the early autumn breeze as she walked to my car still using her cane. When she got inside, I spotted her strappy sandals.

Pat caught my look. "Don't give me any crap. I've been wearing those damn gym shoes for weeks. I'm sick of them!" She scrutinized me from head to toe as I backed the car into the street. "Talk about fancy getups. Red and low cut are reserved for hookers, but it's a good color on you." She whistled low and let her eyes follow my leg line. "I've never seen you with a hemline above your knees." When she got a good look at my foot pressing the accelerator, she pointed to my shoes. "How high are those heels?"

"Four inches and now I'll be taller than you."

"What about your knee?"

"Killing me!"

Pat laughed, "It doesn't matter cause you're looking good!"

I took on the Beltway and headed for the District. Jeffrey Osborne sang softly as I maneuvered through traffic. Pat and I stayed quiet during the drive, both putting our thoughts together. Driving into the heart of the city, I turned on Pennsylvania Avenue toward the White House. When we passed it, I pulled up to the building across the street: The Hay-Adams.

Although I had visited most hotels in the Capitol, I never had the opportunity to enter this mystical place steeped in artistry and history, but reserved for the rich and powerful. Pat and I walked into the elegant lobby and I was not surprised to see Steele dressed in evening attire there to greet us. His dark suit and tie were a rich material, light and shiny like silk.

He greeted us with a warm smile. "Ladies, glad you're here. Let's go upstairs."

We followed him to the elevator and talked about the lovely September weather on our way up. The doors opened to the top floor and he led us to the last door. When Steele knocked, an equally tall and handsome man opened the door, Luc Raines.

Luc looked genuinely happy to see us. "Welcome, ladies. Thank you for coming!" He swung open the door and we entered the lavish suite decorated in French Provincial. Both Pat and I wandered taking in the delicately carved furniture, sumptuous drapery and rich colors.

As if we were exploring a museum, I kept reminding myself not to touch the brush strokes left by the masters on the old canvases. Pat walked up next to me and we both sighed looking at the rich painting depicting life in Paris before their Revolution.

I heard ice being shaken at the tiny bar and smiled at Steele pouring two Cosmopolitans in oversized martini glasses. He winked at me as his long fingers squeezed juice from a lime. Turning back, I caught Pat's wicked smile. She whispered to me, "Could this be any better?"

Steele brought over our drinks and placed them on a gold leaf table. Pointing to the settee behind it, he offered Pat and I a place to sit before he returned to the bar. Pouring two scotch rocks, he put one in front of each white wingback located on either side of us. Finally, Steele sat down on the chair closest to me and Luc sat next to Pat.

We picked up our glasses together, but it was Pat who offered the toast. "To a long and happy relationship!" Everyone agreed and we drank to it.

Sitting back, we engaged in small talk about the storm and the cleanup. It was when Steele got up to refresh our drinks that Luc said, "Our dinner will be another thirty minutes. They're pretty busy downstairs."

Pat spoke up, "That's fine. These drinks are fabulous." She called across the room, "Hey Steele, where'd you learn to make Cosmos?"

"New York, where else?"

I had to ask him, "Is Steele your real name or can you tell us?"

Luc interjected, "Hey Steele, you're popular tonight."

"I'll guess that Steele is your real name?" Pat added, "Since Luc uses it all the time."

He delivered four more drinks to the table and sat down before answering. "Steele was my southern mother's maiden name and she passed her family name down to me as a first name."

Pat piped up, "Nice tradition!"

Luc smiled, "My father passed his first name down to me. I think that's a Connecticut tradition." We all laughed and the light conversation continued until our dinner was delivered.

"This Chateaubriand is delicious." I had to say.

Luc added, "The beef tenderloin might be the heart of this meal, but it is the fresh vegetables cooked delicately that make it one of my favorites."

Steele held up his scotch. "To the French and their illustrious Napoleon."

Bottles of French red wine were brought out and both men discussed European history. They discussed the battle plans of the French wars which made for lively conversation and lots of questions from us.

While I watched and listened, it became apparent that these men hailed from West Point or Annapolis where warfare made up a good part of the curriculum. I could see that Pat was intrigued by their strategic knowledge as well. We sat mesmerized by their many stories.

It was not until the cognac was poured that we began to talk about what had transpired at Barrington Hall. Overflowing with questions, I started. "Is there really a man named Mortez?"

Luc smiled. "Yes, and when that discrete name bounced out on the watch list as being a shipper in the States, I became very curious."

Pat asked, "That's why you took an interest in Barrington Hall?"

"We had also received a back channel message from Poland mentioning Mortez. Once we found out that it supposedly originated from Beck and that one of the places he worked was Barrington Hall, it became obvious that we needed to get someone inside."

I smiled, "Wasn't it lucky that I took a fall that nasty night?"

Steele dropped his head and looked a little ashamed, but Luc nodded. "Yes, we were lucky to get you in there. I'm sorry about your accident, but it was perfect timing."

Steele added, "And when Pat reported the odd things happening around you, we suggested she secure a job there while we dug into the characters living and working inside."

I took another sip of the smooth brandy and let it swish around in my mouth before asking, "What did you find out?"

Luc pointed to Steele who spoke up. "There were a couple of phonies running the place. Not that we could find any criminal intent, but both were working under false names and identification. Talk about master manipulators!" He stopped to smile. "But, I guess you could say they were stars in the marketing arena. Under their reign, they doubled occupancy and cut expenses in half. Their board of directors were so impressed with those numbers, they never delved into their backgrounds."

Pat said, "They had to know they were being investigated. Whatever happened to them?"

Luc answered, "Kyle Marx is still on the storm list as missing. Wilder Wolfe went on vacation and stayed at Meg's house, but never returned."

Steele laughed to himself. "With those soap-opera names, you'd think someone would've looked a little closer into their backgrounds."

Pat chided, "You two should talk. Steele Harris and Luc Raines?" When the two men laughed extremely hard, Pat looked suspicious. "They are your real names, right?" The men passed a silent code to each other, but Pat would not let it go. "C'mon, tell us the truth!"

Steele tried to look sincere. "Only the woman who sees me write my name on our marriage certificate will ever know."

Luc lifted his brandy. "Touche! The same goes for me since we're both still single."

I waited for them to stop joking around before I asked, "Who killed Genevieve?"

Luc cleared his throat, usually the tell of a lie caught in a man's windpipe. "Harold, the boyfriend of your friend, killed Genevieve. Darlene was correct."

"How do you know for sure?"

"It was Harold who climbed into your room and ran down Pat when she chased him."

"Do you know for sure?" I still wanted proof.

Steele cleared his throat this time and I hoped he was not going to lie. "We tracked every SUV that fit the description Pat gave us. One had been stolen in Maryland and our guys found it the day of the storm. It was parked around the corner from Darlene's tavern in Old Town. When we spotted a big guy creeping around the building and climbing the back stairs to the second floor porch, I knew we had him." Steele stopped his narrative to exchange looks with Luc.

"It's okay." Luc waved his hand. "You can tell the girls what happened."

Harold's head hurt and he slept soundly in the back seat as my partner and I drove to Great Falls Park. Lovely place in the early evening. Quiet too, so we could have a private talk."

Pat looked curious. "How'd you get past the gates after sunset?"

Luc smiled, "We're all one, big, happy family in the Federal Government."

"And Harold admitted to the murder?" I asked.

"Oh yes, Harold gave it up. He told us all sorts of things once he got talking. Like how bad he felt that it wasn't his girlfriend bleeding out in Genevieve's bed. And how he had devised a new plan to torture Darlene. He decided to kill off a few more females so Darlene would squirm knowing he was coming for her." Steele stopped and changed his voice to imitate Harold's. "That way she'd be real excited when it came time for her turn."

I felt chills and swallowed more cognac. "That's exactly what Darlene told me, but she thought no one would believe her."

"Harold gave us details, which is why we were going to turn him in to the local police."

"What happened to Harold?" Pat beat me to the question.

"He got away from us and ran. I called out to him. I told him the storm was coming. He kept going. When we caught up to him? That crazy guy was walking across the jagged rocks, trying to get through the white water of the Potomac."

All eyes looked to me for a reaction. "You'll never hear this repeated out of me."

Luc bowed his head. "I'm sure Harold will be memorialized as one of the storm's losses."

Pat added, "Sounds like a happy ending."

Steele got up and refueled our glasses as we mulled over this revelation. It would be doubtful that I would ever see Darlene again, but just in case? I had to tuck away what I had just heard about Harold. Darlene did not need any new nightmares.

The brandy tasted good. It relaxed me and I asked, "There's still a few loose ends."

Luc looked at me. "Let's talk about them."

"Did you hire us to do your dirty work at that Georgetown address?" I asked.

Pat's eyes opened wide as she rolled them between both men, waiting to hear the truth.   Steele sat quiet, as if it was not his turn to confess.

Luc took a long swallow of brandy as he sat contemplating.

The room fell silent. We waited and listened to the ticking of the Louis XV mantel clock.

"I don't have to answer any questions," Luc looked at both of us. "I will because I've never lied to you girls and I want to keep our relationship open and honest." Pat and I nodded.

"Yes, I did send that request to your post office box." He almost looked relieved.

Pat said, "And? Why did you want that man's garbage checked out?"

He smiled at Steele. "Should I tell the girls?"

"Sure, I trust them."

We sent you to Steele's address. It was a test of sorts. You were a new contractor, looking for business, and we wanted to work with you." He turned to Pat. "We liked you from the start."

Steele spoke up, "We had to send you on a trial run."

My mouth was hanging open as I tried to put this information into perspective. "Steele, you're the man who lives alone with Silver?" He smiled and nodded. "And it was you calling him when he ran alongside me in Georgetown?" He nodded again and added a sly smile. "How did the staff at Barrington get acquainted with your dog?"

"I joined a group of volunteers who brought their pets to visit at Barrington Hall. I used it as a cover to get inside and keep an eye on you."

"I don't remember seeing you?"

"You were often sleeping in the beginning. Once, I was walking past your door and almost caught a look at your cute fanny on the commode. Your aide pulled the curtain just in time."

Thoughts of how bad I must have appeared during my first days made me uneasy. "I hope you'll erase those early memories of me. I wasn't in my right mind back then."

"You looked beautiful. You still do and I'm happy to see you up and walking. I felt terrible about your fall. And that wild dog of mine really likes you."

"At the bazaar, it was you dressed as Elvis who called to Silver from the tunnel door?"

"Yes, and I knew he was with you ... hiding."

"Your dog saved us when we were being chased by the escapee dressed like a clown in the tunnel. Silver jumped off my shoulder to bite his nose off." I sighed. "Your dog's very brave."

Steele's eyes beamed and he laughed. "Like father, like son."

Pat was taking this all in, but she was not satisfied. "We still need answers."

Luc looked over at Pat and for the first time, I saw affection in his eyes for her. "Tell me what you need ... I want to make you happy."

She smiled back and returned the tenderness. "Are you trying to take me off subject?"

I jumped at the opportunity to ask, "So this Mortez thing was all a ruse?"

Luc reached out and grabbed the tips of Pat's long fingers hanging off the settee's arm. "Not true. That phantom killer has toyed with us for years. He's an enigma that we've never been able to nail down. The Mossad almost had him a few years ago, but he slipped away."

"What about the information I got from Beck?" When they both began laughing, it made me mad. "Are you mocking me?"

Steele reached over and grabbed my hand. "We have to explain. Beck's disappeared."

I was horrified. "The storm?"

Steele shook his head, but it was Luc who took up the story. "Beck was fifteen when he was turned into an Asset by a CIA handler. That was back in the frozen days of the Cold War. The handler praised the kid and reported how the young man was able to worm his way in and out of secure buildings. Not long after, that handler was murdered and a signature card was left behind supposedly by Mortez. Beck disappeared at the same time and when he resurfaced, told how he was frightened by the killing and ran for cover. We left Beck alone, but kept a back channel of contacts open to him over the years. When he contacted us a couple of years ago, we made it easy for him to get into the country. Not completely trusting Beck, we positioned one of our best Russian operatives up close and personal."

Light bulbs went off in my head. "That would be LuLu?"

Luc nodded and Pat snapped her fingers. "What about that shipping address we found?

Luc shook his head. "Sorry, it was a phony."

Pat frowned, "How do you know that Beck is even the same young man from Poland?"

"We don't," Luc answered. "We didn't use DNA back then."

I jumped off the settee. "You spot check people by their DNA now?"

Steele caught my hand and I sat back when he said, "Maybe?"

Trying to put it all together. "So that's why LuLu kept an eagle eye on Beck."

Luc said, "My guess between us girls? I suspect that Beck is the real Mortez."

Pat looked suspicious. "You think he's been a killer since he's fifteen?"

Luc shrugged his shoulders. "It happens."

Steele added, "We think he's headed overseas to get lost underground in his old world."

Luc smiled, "I have a question for you girls. What's with the potato salad?"

Pat and I laughed, but she explained. "It's code, meaning we're in trouble."

Steele pulled my hand to stand up. "Let's look out at the Capitol by night."

Pat got up. "Me too!" Luc put his arm around her and they followed us. Standing at the windows facing the front of the building, we gazed at that magnificent white building now bathed in lights. The sky was clear and we could almost see the stars twinkle.

Luc must have turned on music because Teddy Pendergrass was singing sweet words of love. Luc led Pat into his arms to dance and she looked happy.

My hands were shaking and I was scared when Steele pulled me into his embrace and we swayed with the music. Following his lead, I relaxed and heard his low voice whisper. "Like riding a bicycle, we never forget some things."

And he was so right. After a few steps, I picked up his rhythm and moved closer until I could smell the delicate scent of his clean shirt ... my favorite aroma.

The four of us danced slow as the men kidded back and forth with each other. Luc kept saying, "We have to be careful with these ladies."

I chimed in, "We break easily!"

Pat yelled, "Come to think of it, I got hurt on the job. How about combat pay?"

Steele laughed, "Me too! I was under stress with all those costume changes." He bent down and kissed the tip of my nose. "And don't forget, I had to deliver the potato salad!"

I kissed him back on the lips and said, "Thank you!"

Luc hugged Pat. "You're wonderful and I promise to make it up to you."

As Luc went to freshen our drinks, the front desk called and advised him that a package had been delivered by courier. He told them to hold it until the morning as he did not want to be disturbed.

The rest of the evening was spent dancing, laughing and ... forgetting.

The End